PERISH IN PARADISE

CHRISTIAN WRIGHT

Copyright © Christian Wright, 2024
All Rights Reserved.

No part of this publication may be reproduced, distributed, or transmitted in any form or by any means, including photocopying, recording, or other electronic or mechanical methods, without the prior written permission of the publisher, except in the case of brief quotations embodied in critical reviews and specific other noncommercial uses permitted by copyright law.

Chapter Images: Cruise Ship@Vecteezy
Format Designer: Dawn Baca

 Created with Vellum

For my grandma Joyce,
For inspiring my sleuth in this book, Iris, with her kind heart, love of family, love of humanity, love of mysteries, and for teaching me that there are still good people in the world.

PROLOGUE

Ten Years Ago
Monday, August 11, 2014

Orlando Print News Report Excerpt

Boating Accident Results in Missing Woman on Lake Granite

Stacy Underwood, a journalist for the *Orlando Gazette* and wife of real estate tycoon Charles Underwood of *Underwood Real Estate*, mysteriously disappeared yesterday on Lake Granite during a boating accident on the Underwood's yacht.
By Nora Brooks

Stacy Underwood, a 40-year-old reporter for the *Orlando Gazette* and wife of real estate tycoon Charles Underwood, disappeared earlier yesterday morning while on her husband's yacht on Lake Granite. The Underwood family had gone out for their annual family outing that morning when the incident occurred. According to the yacht's captain, it hit a UFO (unidentified floating object), causing the yacht to tip. This resulted in people getting thrown overboard. Once the family regrouped, they noticed that Stacy Underwood was missing. After noticing that Stacy Underwood was missing, her husband, Charles, contacted the police, who then launched an investigation to search the lake. However, their initial search was unsuccessful. They only found some clothes Stacy had been wearing before she disappeared. But the police haven't closed their investigation. They issued a BOLO in case Stacy made it ashore farther down the embankment. Stacy Underwood has curly dark brown hair, green eyes, and pale skin; she is 5'4" tall. At the time of her disappearance, she wore a strapless white and blue-colored dress with a floral print, a pair of butterfly earrings, and a mother-of-pearl necklace. Charles Underwood put up a fifty-thousand-dollar reward for anyone who finds and locates his wife alive. The public's help is crucial in this investigation. If anyone has any tips or information regarding locating Stacy Underwood, then please call the hotline.

1

Ten Years Ago
Tuesday, August 12, 2014, Evening

Iris had just finished chopping vegetables on the cutting board when she heard the front door open. She assumed her husband had just gotten home from work. As she scooped the vegetables up and dumped them in the pot on the stove, she said, "Welcome home, honey. How was your day at work?"

A moment later, Henry appeared in the kitchen and exhaled as he said, "Terrible. I've been running around Lake Granite all day trying to locate that missing reporter, Stacy Underwood, to no avail. If you ask me, her no-good husband Charles somehow got rid of her."

Iris's eyebrow rose in curiosity as she continued to cook dinner. She poured salt and pepper into the pot and asked, "Why do you say that?"

Henry laughed as he said, "Charles Underwood is one of the biggest real estate tycoons in the South. Plus, rumor has it he was having an affair. Perhaps his wife was threatening to file for divorce. So, he kills her to avoid splitting his wealth with her."

"I can see your point," Iris replied. "That seems like a classic tale of a rich man wanting to get rid of his spouse to keep his wealth to himself. But you said something about there being rumors of an affair. Do you know who Charles supposedly had an affair with or if it's connected to Stacy's disappearance?"

Henry frowned as he said, "It depends on who you ask. There are several rumors. Some say he was cheating on his wife with someone he worked with. Others say it was someone he was showing houses to. While others claim he picked some young thing up at a bar. But we don't even know if he was cheating or if it's connected to the case. The whole situation is so frustrating. My boss is demanding I wrap up this case ASAP because of the status of the people involved."

Iris stirred the pot and lowered the temperature before saying, "I know it's frustrating, honey. The status of the people involved in the case shouldn't force you to work faster. Everyone's case should be treated the same regardless of how rich they are or who they know."

Henry laughed, saying, "I wish that were the case, but you know how politics work. The rich run the world and get top priority. Meanwhile, Charles's administrative assistant's case is getting put on the back burner."

This caused Iris's eyebrow to raise as she said, "What happened to Charles's administrative assistant?"

Henry approached his wife and said, "Someone killed her last Friday in a hit-and-run. However, they consider her case a lower priority since she is a foreigner. I know it's not right, but there isn't much I can do about it."

Once he reached his wife, Henry hugged her from behind. Iris turned her head in surprise as he kissed her before continuing, "But enough about that for now. What are we having for dinner?"

Iris laughed at Henry's inability to tell what she was

cooking despite having been married for almost twenty-five years.

"Chicken noodle soup. It should be ready soon," she said in response.

Henry's face lit up as he laughed and said, "Well, it smells wonderful. I think I'm going to shower real quick while it finishes cooking. See you in a few minutes, babe," he said before grabbing another quick kiss.

Iris grinned before pretending to slap him and saying, "Go now, or I'll never finish dinner."

Henry stepped away and held his hands up in mock defeat, saying, "Yes, ma'am," before heading to the bathroom and leaving Iris to finish cooking dinner.

2

Present Day
Friday, August 9, 2024, 10:00 a.m.

As Iris stood outside a dimly lit tunnel, a sense of unease washed over her. The light at the end was barely visible, shrouded in a mysterious haze. A sudden, chilling breeze from the tunnel made her shiver, and she instinctively crossed her arms over her chest. Then, out of nowhere, a blinding ball of light materialized in front of her. As the light dimmed, she saw the figure of her late husband, Henry. A mix of emotions flooded her, and she couldn't help but ask, "What are you doing here?"

"Beware of false illusions if you wish to find the truth. Things are not always what they appear to be."

Iris stood confused as she said, "What do you mean? Beware of false illusions if I want to find the truth. What truth am I looking for?" However, she heard a loud, familiar beeping sound before she could get an answer. Her dream was abruptly interrupted, and it brought her back to reality.

Iris opened her eyes and stretched as she turned off her phone alarm. What a strange dream, she thought as she got out of bed. Iris wondered if her late husband was trying to warn her of something yet to come or if she was overthinking the whole thing. She shook her head at the thought. Henry had been dead for almost five years now. Why would he show up now? Besides, what could he be trying to warn her about? It definitely was not the cruise she was going on today. Iris laughed at her inner discussion about her dream. She wondered if she was going crazy being alone all the time now.

As Iris rose from her bed, a pang of emptiness washed over her. The absence of Henry's morning presence was a constant reminder of her loss. She pushed the feeling aside, determined to focus on the present. Today was a day for new experiences, and she wasn't going to let the past dampen her spirits. With a resolute smile, she began preparing for her cruise.

After showering, Iris packed all her clothes and toiletries into her travel bag. Then she located her passport, boarding pass, and the necessary paperwork to board the cruise later and put those in her bag.

Once she had finished packing, Iris went and made a pot of coffee and cooked herself some breakfast. After finishing, Iris made her plate, poured some coffee, and sat at the kitchen table. As she ate breakfast, Iris picked up today's newspaper and flipped through it. The front-page headline caught her attention as she read the *Tenth anniversary of Stacy Underwood's mysterious disappearance*. Iris felt surprised to see that old name again. It brought back images of her late husband coming home from long shifts trying to locate the missing woman, interviewing suspects, and following leads to no avail. Iris wondered what happened to Stacy Underwood as she finished her breakfast. Guess nobody would ever know, she thought as she picked up her dirty plate, scraped it, and put it in the sink before returning to the kitchen table.

A few moments later, Iris finished her coffee and went to the sink with her dirty plate and empty coffee cup. After washing the dishes, she dried them before returning them to the proper place. Once finished, she checked the time on the stove. It read 11:15 a.m. It was almost time to leave if she wanted to get to port at noon. She did a walk-through, checking to make sure everything was in place. Once satisfied with her last inspection and her bags safely tucked into the trunk of the car. She locked up the house and set off.

After parking her car on the fourth floor of the parking garage, she removed her travel bags from the trunk and walked to the service elevator. Once on the ground floor, Iris exited the parking garage and headed towards the port.

The SS Paradise, a majestic sight, stood before her. Its white hull stretched across the water like a giant, its deckhouse and superstructures reaching for the sky. The ship's name, boldly displayed, seemed to call out to her. As she waited in line, a sense of anticipation and excitement filled her. This was a feeling she had not experienced in a long time.

As she approached the cruise terminal, Iris noticed some men dressed in colorful, festive clothing guarding the entrance to the ship. The line to get on the SS Paradise was already quite long, so Iris got in line and waited her turn.

A short while later, her turn came. A staff member asked to see her passport and other boarding papers. After retrieving the documents from her carry-on bag, Iris presented them to the worker. Barely glancing at them, the worker returned them to Iris, who quickly returned them to her carry-on bag before being directed to the security line.

Once there, Iris had to place her carry-on bag and luggage through an X-ray machine as she walked through a metal detector. After proving she had no weapons or contraband, Iris retrieved her carry-on. Then, Iris walked to another line where a staff member made her fill out a health form stating she hadn't been ill or had shown no signs of feeling unwell recently.

After completing the health form, the attentive worker carefully checked it. Once satisfied with the results, the worker took Iris's picture for her cruise card, adding a personal touch to the check-in process. A few moments later, Iris received her cruise card, room key, and onboard credit card, a gesture that made her feel welcomed and valued, before proceeding up the gangway.

3

Present Day
Friday, August 9, 2024, 1:00 p.m.

Nora just entered the atrium of the SS Paradise. She was in awe of the sight before her as she explored the open area. The atrium had majestic soaring ceilings that seemed to go on forever, thanks to the atmospheric LED lights that shone from the ceiling and hit the dazzling crystal chandeliers that hung overhead. On the walls of the atrium was an assortment of well-crafted abstract art pieces mixed in with some tasteful landscape portraits. There was also a surprising number of marble statues scattered around strategically placed locations. The overall result was a feeling of undeniable wealth. Nora felt out of her element here, like an outsider who somehow slipped into a VIP party unannounced. Fortunately for Nora, she won that contest in the mail that won her a free trip aboard this cruise ship; otherwise, there was no way she could have afforded this trip. The thought filled her with slight envy at the sight of all these rich, well-to-do people who stood around here who could casually afford this trip like it was nothing. Not that she could complain, Nora reasoned. She could have had that life but chose not to. Sometimes, she wondered if she had made the right choice back then. The thought made Nora feel nostalgic, but she tried to shake off the feeling. She lived for the present now, not what could have been or once was. Nora thought a distraction was what she needed. So, she explored all the various decks of the atrium to see what the ship offered.

As Nora began making her rounds, she noticed the ship had everything one could want. On deck seven, she noticed a library and some cozy cafes, which could work as a nice, quiet lunch spot, she mused. Going up to the next floor to deck eight, Nora found an assortment of restaurants, which she guessed would be where she would have her dinners for the next week. Nora appreciated the variety they sported. She saw an Italian restaurant, a Mexican, Soul Food, and a Japanese restaurant to boot. Nora already knew she had to try each and do an online review for her blog as she continued to the next floor.

On deck nine, she located the pool, lounge, and bar. Nora knew she would spend a lot of time on this part of the ship. She could swim a few laps in the pool or lay out and read that contemporary crime novel she received for her birthday. The thought sounded delightful as she continued her exploration.

On deck ten, she spotted a salon and a spa, a haven for self-care. It also housed a gym, a place she hadn't stepped foot in for years. The sight brought a wistful smile to her face, a reminder of a different time in her life. She doubted if she would start going on a luxury cruise, but the sight was a pleasant one. There was nothing else of interest on this floor, so she tried to go up to the next floor but noticed that the door read, Bridge area, *For Employees Only*. Guess I need to turn around then, reasoned Nora, so she returned to where she started. But as she headed back to deck six, Nora spotted an old ghost from her past sitting at the bar on deck nine, sipping on a pina colada. The sight sent a jolt of anxiety through her, her heart racing. As a matter of reflex, she unzipped her bag, pulled out her prescription, popped one of her pills, and swallowed, trying to calm her nerves.

Of course, *she* would be here, Nora thought. The universe had to test her somehow for winning that contest for this free cruise she didn't deserve. Nora couldn't handle this right now. She needed to go lay down and rest, so she searched for her cabin on one of the ship's lower decks.

4

Present Day
Friday, August 9, 2024, 1:30 p.m.

Sandy was sitting in the lounge area on deck nine, sipping a cold one. It looked like he was just a man who wanted to get started on his day drinking on his vacation. However, the truth was far from it. He was actually on a stakeout for a woman named Nora. Although his luck so far has been far from fruitful, alas, the day was still young, and he still had an entire week to get the job done. So, for now, he planned to relax and enjoy his beer in peace. He rarely got hired to go on a cruise to tail someone, and it was even less frequent for the client to cover such an expense. However, this case seemed to differ from his usual requests, especially since his client was the real estate tycoon Charles Underwood.

Sandy didn't particularly like his client's unsavory background, but he had bills to pay and desperately needed cash. Plus, he was confident this job was going to be cake. All he had to do was to determine if Nora Brooks had any knowledge or connection to Charles's missing or, should he say, deceased wife, Stacy, since it's been ten years since her disappearance, and now she was legally considered dead. Sandy couldn't understand why Charles had this crazy notion that this Nora person had any new information on this matter. From as far as he could tell, the two women had no connections whatsoever, minus the fact they were both reporters who worked in Orlando ten years ago when Stacy mysteriously disappeared from that boating accident on Lake Granite. Sandy thought Charles was probably just a man who missed his wife and was suffering from being able to move on. Or maybe the man felt guilty for how he had treated his wife back then and wanted to repay her memory somehow. Sandy remembered some of the nasty rumors going around back then concerning Charles Underwood. Maybe this was his karma, Sandy thought as he finished his beer. Regardless, he guessed he needed to track down this Nora person. But then again, thought Sandy, why rush when there was probably nothing to report, anyway? So, instead, Sandy got up and got in line for another beer.

5

Present Day
Friday, August 9, 2024, 1:45 p.m.

Charles Underwood, a man of considerable means, had just arrived at the atrium of the SS Paradise. He couldn't help but feel a twinge of impatience at the sight of the long queues. Not a man accustomed to waiting in line with the common folk. The purpose of his wealth and status, he pondered, was to make life more comfortable. With this thought in mind, he set out to explore the cruise's offerings.

Charles was happy that the cruise had a plethora of eye candy to satisfy his hunger. If he played his cards right this week, he could score. The thought was enticing. It had been too long since he had enjoyed someone's company, and Charles thought he would have to change that. But first, he needed a little liquid courage to help loosen him up, so Charles searched for the bar.

After locating the bar on deck nine, he noticed a beautiful red-haired girl sitting at the bar sipping a drink, chatting away with a well-dressed blonde-haired man sitting beside her. They looked like a power couple as they bantered back and forth, lost in their own little world. The sight made Charles miss that feeling of connecting with someone on that level. It also made him slightly envious of the couple because it reminded him of the old days with Stacy. Back when things were easy, and he had the world at his feet. If only he could go back in time and change things. If only things were that simple, Charles thought. But life was cruel and unforgiving, as he learned. He knew it wouldn't change anything, but a drink sounded good to Charles, so he went and sat down at the other end of the bar and ordered a drink, hoping it would drown down the painful memories of the past.

6

Present Day
Friday, August 9, 2024, 2:30 p.m.

Selina sat on deck nine on the pool's edge while sipping her tequila sunrise. She had a light buzz going as she saw her fiancé, his muscular frame glistening in the sun, swimming laps in the pool. She admired his tight swimsuit as he swam from one end of the pool to the other. The sight reminded Selina that life could be good sometimes as she sat there soaking her feet in the pool.

A few moments later, Jordan swam over to where Selina was sitting and said, "What's going on, babe? Are you enjoying our vacation so far?"

Selina's face lit up with a radiant smile as she turned to Jordan, her eyes sparkling with gratitude. "Yes, I am. I'm just so incredibly thankful that we won that contest. It's like a dream come true, a luxury we could never have afforded otherwise."

Jordan smiled back at her and said, "Yeah, you're right. It's a good day to be on such a fancy cruise like this with you. I wonder how much it would normally cost."

Selina stroked her chin as she pondered an answer to Jordan's question. After using her financial skills to come up with a quick estimate, she said, "Probably several thousand a piece, be my guess. It's a good thing we had luck on our side and got our tickets for free."

Jordan's eyes sparkled with excitement as he climbed out of the pool and sat by Selina. "I agree. On a different note, I can't wait to go back to our cabin and change clothes. You can join me if you want," he said with a playful wink before standing up.

Selina blushed and said, "Sounds good to me, love," before getting up and joining him. A moment later, the two headed back to their cabin. But as they were doing so, Selina's eyes glimpsed a figure at the bar, someone she thought she recognized. Her face turned slightly pale for a second, but when she looked again, the person was gone. Selina wondered if she had imagined the whole thing since she had been drinking earlier and still had a light buzz. That must be it, she reasoned, and she continued to follow Jordan to her cabin.

7

Present Day
Friday, August 9, 2024, 3:30 p.m.

Georgia sat in a plush salon chair on deck ten, next to her best friend Tyler, who was under the hair dryers.

As they waited for their hair to dry, Georgia admired the salon's elegant design: rich, wooden paneled floors, luxurious, red-colored leather chairs, grand dressing mirrors surrounded by soft, glowing lights, and shelves of high-end products stacked beside them.

Georgia loved to look at the layout of different restaurants and businesses and analyze why the designer used specific colors for materials or why they chose to layout a room a certain way. Because of her fashion major, Georgia saw these situations as works of art and loved trying to understand the thought that went into the finished product. But her thoughts got interrupted by her friend Tyler saying, "Are you doing okay, girlfriend? I've been trying to get your attention for a hot minute, but you were staring off into space."

Georgia laughed as she said, "Sorry, sweetheart, I just got distracted by the ambiance of this salon. You know we don't have fancy things like this back in Orlando. At least not for our pay grade."

Tyler, always the dramatic one, threw his head back and exclaimed, "You got that right, sister. I feel like I'm living out my fairytale, enjoying a self-care day like this with you. Although I'm sure, our wallets will hurt after this trip. But we only live once, and I'm going to make the most of this vacation, especially since we won it for free."

Georgia smiled, saying, "Yes, lucky we won that contest, or we wouldn't be here right now. But I agree with you, sugar. We should enjoy it instead of trying to look a gift horse in the mouth."

Tyler smiled back at his friend and said, "That's what I plan to do. Eat, drink, hang out with you, and try to see if I can find a cute boy to hang out with this week. Speaking of cute boys," Tyler began with a playful smile as he pointed to one of the hair stylists working in the far corner on the other side of the salon. "He is cute."

Georgia laughed at her friend's never-ending quest for love. She glanced over at the hairstylist to check out whom Tyler had his eye on. The man in question was tall, with short dark chestnut hair and little gray flecks mixed in. The image reminded her of someone from the past, and her face turned red momentarily. Tyler noticed this and said, "Are you all right, girlfriend? You seemed to get upset when I pointed out that guy. Is there a story there?"

Georgia blushed at getting caught but quickly replied, "It's nothing. It reminded me of someone I had a bad date with a while back. But it doesn't matter, sugar. He is cute. You should ask him for his number. He might be interested."

This caused Tyler to blush as he said, "I'll have to think about it," but before he could continue, the hair stylists working on their hair returned and told them it was time to finish their appointment, interrupting the conversation.

8

Present Day
Friday, August 9, 2024, 4:00 p.m.

After doing the cruise ship's muster safety drill, Iris just reached her cabin. Overall, the instructions were simple, and Iris wasn't concerned. It was slightly annoying, but she knew the drill was necessary in case of an emergency. She was glad to have the drill over because that signaled that the cruise ship was about to embark on its journey. The thought excited her since it officially signaled the start of her vacation. But in the meantime, she wanted to unpack her luggage. So Iris unlocked the door to her cabin and entered.

Stepping into her cabin, its beauty and comfort immediately struck Iris. The gray tiled floors, the matching-colored sofa, and the small glass coffee table all added to the cozy atmosphere. In the back corner, she discovered a small bathroom with a walk-in shower, and in the kitchen, a stylish oak bar with a microwave, mini fridge, and matching-colored bar stools caught her eye.

The bedroom was on the other side of the wall,

connected to the kitchen. It had a large flat-screen TV hanging on the wall. Directly past it was a big queen-sized bed, already made up. Beside the bed was Iris's luggage bag. As she placed her carry-on bag on the floor, she noticed a note on the nightstand beside the bed. She picked up the small paper pad and read the note. "Greetings, Mrs. May. I hope you find the room to your liking. Later today, the cabin stewardess will come by to drop off a complimentary bottle of champagne and an itinerary detailing the layout of the ship, plus a list of each day's set activities. If you need any room service or would like to make a special request, please call this number, and the stewardess will do her best to honor it."

Iris thought a complimentary bottle of champagne sounded nice, so she returned the note to the nightstand before picking up bags and unpacking some things.

A short while later, Iris unpacked some of the small objects she had brought onboard from the house. The room felt cozier, with her mystery novel lying on her nightstand and her reading glasses on top of it. She also placed a can of her favorite brand of coffee on her kitchen bar. To finish, Iris put her worn-out Bible, which her Aunt Amelia gave her as a wedding present, on the coffee table and the rosary she got when her mother passed away on top of it. The sight made Iris feel somber, but it was a mixture of bitter-sweet feelings of familiarity and loss. But as Iris reflected on what was and still is, she heard the intercom come on and say, "Good afternoon, everyone; this is your captain speaking. I hope everyone is doing well. We are about to leave port soon, and as usual, we will host a sail-away party to commemorate our departure. This event will take place on deck nine in fifteen minutes. There will be drinks at the bar, a pool party, and a DJ playing music. We will also offer song requests. I hope everyone will come to celebrate this event with us. Until then, take care, everyone."

She couldn't help but feel a surge of excitement at the

thought of the sail-away party. But before she could join in the fun on deck nine, she had to change into her swimming attire.

9

Present Day
Friday, August 9, 2024, 5:00 p.m.

Nora just arrived on deck nine for the sail-away party. She had been debating whether to attend, but she reasoned many people would be there, so, with any luck, she wouldn't run into that woman from the past again.

As Nora surveyed the scene, the chorus of Taylor Swift's *Cruel Summer* was playing in the background. A long line had formed at the bar, and the pool was a sea of people in skin-tight swimwear, jumping and swimming. The sight, reminiscent of her youth, beauty, and desirability, left a bitter taste in her mouth. Deciding a drink was in order, she joined the line at the bar.

After what felt like an eternity, Nora ordered a fruity sangria. Receiving her drink, Nora reached for her onboard credit card when somebody behind her said, "Excuse me, bartender. I would like to pay for the lady's drink."

Nora jumped at the surprise as she turned around to see who was trying to pay for her drink. The sight was a roguishly handsome man, with deep blue eyes and a five o'clock shadow, holding out his card. Nora watched the bartender take the card, swipe it, and ask him if he wanted anything himself. The mystery man ordered a beer. While the bartender went to fetch it, the man turned to Nora, smiled at her, and said, "My bad, I forgot to introduce myself. My name is Sandy. What is your name, beautiful?"

Nora laughed at the whole situation. She was almost fifty years old, and a man who looked closer to his thirties was trying to pick her up. Feeling flattered but wary of bad news, she said, "My name is Nora, and thanks for buying my drink, but I have business to attend to. So, I'm going to take my drink and head out. Have a nice day, Sandy." Then Nora tried to leave. At first, it seemed like he was trying to follow her, but he quickly gave up. Nora breathed a sigh of relief as she headed to the pool. It was time to enjoy her drink, relax, and enjoy her vacation without any creeps or past trauma pestering her. This was going to be her week, she thought as she arrived at the pool with sangria in hand.

10

Present Day
Friday, August 9, 2024, 5:15 p.m.

The loud blast of noise coming from the music the DJ was playing and the horde of people scattered around the deck immediately caught her attention as Iris arrived on deck nine. The overall mood made her feel slightly uncomfortable. Iris knew she probably would only stay here briefly because of her introverted nature, but that wouldn't stop her from having a good time. Plus, she had a new swimsuit on and wanted to break it in, so she headed to the pool.

The pool, a glistening oasis amidst the bustling deck, beckoned with its crystal-clear waters and a bottom painted in a vibrant shade of blue. The scent of chlorine, though slightly stinging Iris's nose, was a testament to the pool's cleanliness. A multitude of people, spanning various ages, filled the pool, some swimming, others dipping their feet, some jumping in, and a few lounging nearby. The atmosphere was one of pure joy, and the sight brought a smile to Iris's face as she joined in, dipping her feet into the pool.

As Iris sat, her feet immersed in the cool water, she

couldn't help but be drawn to the young couple playfully splashing each other. Their laughter echoed in her ears, triggering a flood of memories of her and Henry in their youth. The nostalgia was bittersweet, a reminder of a time long gone. But Iris had no regrets, and as she looked around, her gaze fell on a beautiful older woman enjoying her solitude by the poolside.

The woman looked closer to Iris's age than most of the people Iris had seen on this cruise so far. Iris wondered if she should go over and introduce herself to the woman. After a moment of hesitation, Iris stood and headed toward the woman on the other side of the pool. But on her way over there, a man caught her eye. For a moment, Iris felt extreme shock. Standing in the distance, sipping a beer, was Charles Underwood.

What is he doing here? Iris wondered in shock. She felt a mixture of anger and pain at the sight of him. It reminded her of sleepless nights when her husband worked on Stacy Underwood's missing cold case, to no avail. A headache started developing, and Iris decided she needed to lie down and process the image of that horrible man she had just seen. So, she retrieved her bag and returned to her room in a daze.

11

Ten Years Ago
Tuesday, August 19, 2014, Evening

Iris, a woman of routine, filled up the pan with water before placing it on the stove. Then she turned the temperature to high and sprinkled some salt into the pan. While waiting for the water to boil, she turned on her countertop TV. A moment later, Nancy Grace appeared on the screen. The headline below read, *Real Estate Tycoon's Wife Disappearance: Accident or Murder?* Iris wondered the same thing as she listened to Nancy give updates on Stacy Underwood's disappearance. Most of the information was stuff Iris already knew since her husband, Henry, was the lead detective on the case. Nancy talked about how Stacy had been a well-known reporter for the *Orlando Print* for the past ten years and how her husband was the infamous tycoon Charles Underwood of *Underwood Real Estate*. Nancy brought up an interesting point about the odd coincidence that Charles's administrative assistant, Inga Lagman, had died in a hit-and-run just a few days before Stacy mysteriously disappeared.

There was a lot of speculation regarding the connection between the two events. Iris wasn't sure herself, but the timing was odd for sure. It made her wonder what other kinds of trouble Charles Underwood had gotten himself into as she checked the water. It was boiling, so she turned the heat down before she poured the pasta into the pan.

A few moments later, Iris heard the front door creak open. A smile, like a ray of sunshine, came to her face at the thought of her husband arriving home for work, so she went to the fridge and pulled out a pound of hamburger. Then she placed the hamburger on a plate, put it in the microwave, and hit the defrost button before saying, "Welcome home, honey. How was work today?"

Henry stepped into the kitchen and said, "Stressful. I've been out interviewing people connected to Charles Underwood and his wife, Stacy. However, I'm still no closer to uncovering the truth regarding her disappearance." His voice was heavy with frustration, and Iris could see the lines of worry etched on his face.

Iris grabbed a large spoon to stir her noodles as she said, "That sounds like a headache, dear. Why don't you tell me all about it?"

Henry sighed as he sat down at the kitchen table and said, "Sure, why not?" before he continued, "Today, I went and interviewed Charles's intern, Clara, about whether she had any information regarding the rumors about Charles having an affair or anything related to the death of Charles's administrative assistant, Inga. But Clara claimed she knew nothing about Charles cheating on his wife or if he was involved in Inga's death. So, that was a failure."

The timer on the microwave dinged, so she retrieved the hamburger. After removing it from its packaging, she placed it in another pan on the stove. She turned up the heat before saying, "Are you sure this intern wasn't lying about having any knowledge about Inga or Charles having an affair? Is it possible she might be the one he was having an affair with?"

Henry laughed as he said, "I don't think so. From my understanding of things, Clara is a lesbian. So, I don't think she would have an affair with Charles. And as for her lying, I can't see why she would."

Iris stirred her hamburger as it sizzled, filling the kitchen with a mouthwatering aroma. Then she stirred her pasta before pulling one out to taste. It tasted delightful, the perfect al dente. So, she turned the water on low before saying, "I see your point. It seems like a dead end. Who else did you interview today, then?"

Henry leaned back in his chair as he said, "I also questioned Inga's daughter, Selina. I wanted to ask her if she knew if her mom had any enemies or if her mom suspected Charles of having an affair or any other shady dealings. Selina stated her mom had mentioned Charles cheating before, and she firmly believes that Charles was involved in her mom's death."

Iris stirred the hamburger and noticed that it was turning brown, so she turned down the heat before saying, "That's interesting. Did Selina give you examples of what her mother told her about the cheating?"

Henry got up from his chair and walked over to Iris before saying, "Yes, she did. But I'll get to that later. I'm about to go shower and freshen up. But first, tell me what that yummy smell is coming from the stove?"

Iris laughed at her husband as she said, "It's spaghetti and meat sauce, goofball. And it should be ready soon."

Henry's eyes lit up as he got up and hugged her from behind. Iris turned around and smiled before kissing her husband. After the quick embrace, Henry said, "Well, it smells fantastic. Almost as good as you."

Iris playfully slapped Henry as she said, "Yeah, yeah, Casanova. You only married me for my cooking."

Henry blushed as he said, "That's not the only reason. However, it definitely was a deciding factor."

Iris shook her head before saying, "Go take your shower so I can finish cooking in peace."

Henry nodded as he said, "Yes, ma'am," before returning to the bathroom. Iris laughed at her husband before she turned around and finished cooking their dinner.

12

Present Day
Friday, August 9, 2024, 5:30 p.m.

Selina was sitting next to her fiancé, Jordan, on the lounge of deck nine, enjoying the sail-away party. As she sipped her pina colada, Selina listened to Jordan sing *Best Day of My Life* in an off-key tone. Selina laughed internally at the sight of it. She couldn't believe that she and he would be married in less than a year from now. Where had the time gone? Selina wondered as she took another sip of her drink. But she noticed the cup was almost empty. So, she looked at Jordan and said, "Hi honey, could you please be a dear and go get me another drink?"

Jordan turned to face Selina, smiled, and said, "For sure, babe," before getting up and heading to the bar.

It felt like an eternity since Jordan left for the bar, and Selina's worry gnawed at her. She debated whether to look for him when Jordan suddenly appeared with her drink. But something was off. His face looked pale as he handed her a drink. Before she could ask, Jordan said, "You wouldn't believe who I saw while getting your drink."

Selina panicked as she waited for Jordan to confirm her fears. "Charles Underwood. Isn't it crazy we would run into him after all these years?"

Selina felt like she would be sick as she said, "It sure is. I might have seen him earlier today, but I hoped I was mistaken. I know it's wrong of me to say, but I wish he weren't here. Someone like him doesn't deserve to enjoy nice things like this cruise. You know I have bad blood with him." Her voice trembled with a mix of fear and anger, her emotions threatening to spill over.

Jordan's touch was warm and comforting as he grabbed Selina's hand. His voice was steady, reassuring. "I know you are upset that he's here. It upsets me as well. But there isn't much we can do about it. So, we must try not to let it ruin our vacation."

Selina took a deep breath, her voice filled with resignation. "I know you're right, dear. There is no way we could have guessed that he would be here. But it just doesn't seem fair. But like you said, there isn't much we can do. So, we might as well enjoy ourselves."

Jordan smiled at Selina before saying with a wink, "Good idea. I think I got an idea that will make you feel better."

Selina laughed as she said, "Oh yeah. What is on your mind?"

Jordan smiled mischievously as he said, "Follow me and find out," before pulling Selina along with him.

13

Present Day
Friday, August 9, 2024, 5:45 p.m.

Georgia, her heart light with the joy of the sail-away celebration, was humming along to the beat of the music. Her best friend, Tyler, was singing *Sail Away*, a sight that brought a smile to her face. But the ship's intercom, its voice breaking through the air, interrupted their bliss. "Good evening, everyone. This is your captain speaking. I hope everyone has enjoyed the sail-away party so far. I just wanted to let you know this event will end in fifteen minutes, so please finish what you're doing there. At this time, the restaurants on deck eight will start serving food until 10 p.m. So, please make sure you eat before then. Otherwise, I wish everyone a good first day of sailing."

As the captain finished speaking, Georgia glanced at Tyler and said, "I think we should get ready for dinner. What is your opinion, Ty?"

Tyler, his face alight with a mischievous grin, said, "Sounds good to me, GG. Let's get out of here." With a swift motion, he rose from his lounge chair, and Georgia, her movements mirroring his, got up as well. Then, the two embarked on their journey back to their rooms.

On their way back, Tyler spoke slowly, saying, "I think I may have seen Charles Underwood a moment ago. Yet, I cannot be sure."

Georgia felt anger creeping in as she questioned, "Where?"

Tyler pointed over to a group of people at the bar and said, "He's the one in the blue button-up shirt."

Georgia's eyes darted across the room, her gaze settling on a figure in a blue button-up shirt. It was Charles Underwood, a sight that ignited a fire within her. "Well, I'm fit to be tied. You're right. Here he is!" she exclaimed, her voice laced with a mix of anger and surprise.

Tyler spoke cautiously, saying, "I'm sorry. I know you have bad blood with him, and I wasn't trying to tell you, GG. However, I went into a state of shock when I saw him."

Georgia's mind was set. She was determined to steer clear of Charles, no matter the size of the ship. She was relieved to learn of his presence, as it gave her a chance to prepare.

"Don't worry, Ty. We'll manage. Let's try our best to avoid him, and everything will be fine. Let's focus on getting ready for dinner."

Tyler's worry was evident as he asked, "Are you sure you're okay, GG? I'm here for you, you know."

Georgia nodded her head before saying, "Yes, I'm sure. Now, let's go, honey."

Tyler sighed and said, "Okay," before the two resumed their journey back to their rooms to prepare for dinner.

14

Present Day
Friday, August 9, 2024, 6:00 p.m.

Iris had just arrived on deck eight of the cruise ship, which housed all the major restaurants. She was looking at her options, trying to decide where she wanted to eat. From the look of things, there was an Italian restaurant, a Mexican, Soul Food, and a Japanese one. They all sounded good, but Iris thought a plate of pasta sounded best, so she approached the Italian restaurant.

Once inside the cozy Italian restaurant, Iris's nose was immediately greeted by a delicious aroma of Italian breadsticks, freshly baked spaghetti and meatballs, and homemade pizza. The smell brought a smile to her face, and she eagerly anticipated her dinner as she waited in line to be seated, taking in the warm, inviting atmosphere of the restaurant.

A few moments later, Iris reached the host's stand. The host asked how many, and Iris replied, "Table for one." The host then grabbed a menu and led Iris to her table. While she waited for her server to arrive, Iris looked over the menu.

About ten minutes later, a server arrived and took Iris's

drink order and what she wanted to eat before running off. Now bored, Iris looked around to see who she could spot sitting at the other tables. She mostly spotted younger couples scattered about the various tables, with a few singles sprinkled here and there. One, in particular, caught her eye. Sitting in the far corner, reading a book, sat a woman who looked like the one Iris was going to approach earlier today at the pool. What were the odds they would end up eating in the same place for dinner? Iris wondered if she should go introduce herself. But she quickly rejected the idea since the woman was busy reading her book when she noticed a man approach the woman in question. Heat rose to Iris's face when she realized the man was none other than Charles Underwood.

Iris focused her gaze on the interaction between Charles and the mystery woman in the corner. The woman looked uncomfortable, and Iris was debating getting help when the server suddenly returned with her drink. Iris looked at the server as she said, "That woman over there in the corner looks to be in distress." Then, she pointed at the woman and continued, "Could you please go check on her and see if she's all right?" She couldn't stand by and do nothing, not when someone might be in trouble.

The server looked at where Iris was pointing and said, "Sure thing, Miss," before taking off in that direction. Iris watched the scene unfold, her heart pounding in her chest. The server got Charles to leave but heard him shout something at the woman before stomping off. A wave of relief washed over Iris as she realized she had made a difference.

A moment later, the server returned smiling before saying, "It's all taken care of, Miss. Thanks for the tip."

Iris murmured, "No problem."

The server smiled and said, "I'll be back with your food shortly," before taking off.

After the server left, the mystery woman approached Iris's table and said, "Sorry to bother you, but that server said you had him come over and help me out of that sticky situation a moment ago, and I just wanted to give my thanks."

Iris smiled as she said, "It's no problem. I recognized that man and knew he was bad news, so I wanted to help if possible." She couldn't help but feel a sense of satisfaction at having potentially averted a dangerous situation.

The woman turned slightly pale as she said, "You recognized that man. Who is he?"

As Iris spoke to the woman, she pointed out, "That's Charles Underwood, the real estate tycoon." To her slight surprise, the woman didn't recognize him. Iris further added, "You might also remember him as the man whose wife disappeared ten years ago." She couldn't help but feel a mix of curiosity and concern about the woman's reaction.

The woman's mouth fell open as she said, "I remember who he is now. It's scary that he approached me a minute ago. But I've gotten off track and forgot to introduce myself. My name is Nora Brooks," she said, her voice trembling slightly.

That name felt familiar to Iris, but she couldn't place it as she said, "Nice to meet you, Nora. My name is Iris May. You're more than welcome to join me for dinner."

"That's sweet of you, but I don't want to intrude."

"You're not intruding, dear. But I understand if you want to return to your table and finish reading."

After a moment of hesitation, Nora said, "Well, okay. Let me get my book and drink, and I'll join you."

Iris smiled and said, "Sounds good," before watching Nora return to her table to retrieve her stuff.

15

Ten Years Ago
August 9, 2014

Orlando Print News Report Excerpt

Local Real Estate Administrative Assistant Killed in a Hit and Run on Old River Road

Last night, someone fatally hit Inga Lagman, an administrative assistant for real estate tycoon Charles Underwood, in a hit-and-run on *Old River Road*. They found Inga's totaled car on the side of the road. Reports indicate that someone hit the car from behind, but no other vehicles were seen when it was reported.
By Nora Brooks

A jogger discovered the body of Inga Lagman, a 38-year-old mother of one and the administrative assistant for *Underwood Real Estate*, on *Old River Road* last night from a hit and run. A jogger who had seen the car lying in a ditch on the side of the road reported the crime. Police are calling the incident foul play because someone hit the vehicle from behind and pushed it off the road. However, there are currently no leads in this unfortunate case. Inga Lagman had worked for *Underwood Real Estate* for several years while being a single parent to her only child, Selina, a junior in high school.

When asked if her mom had any enemies, her daughter said, "My mom was one of the most selfless people I ever met. She gave up everything to move here and give me a better life. She was and still is my hero. I can't think of anyone who would wish to harm her except maybe her boss, Charles Underwood. My mom told me he had a bad temper." When Inga's former employer was asked for comment, he said, "It is a sad day for us all. Inga was a very valuable employee in my service for many years. I am sorry that her daughter thinks I had something to do with her death. But since she is grieving, I will overlook her comments. But I want everyone to know that Inga was family, and I hope they find out who did this."

The public's help is crucial in this investigation. If anyone has any tips or information regarding this case, please call the hotline to help solve this case. Services for Inga Lagman will be at *Austin's* on *Old Silver Road* this Saturday if you wish to pay your respects.

16

Present Day
Friday, August 9, 2024, 6:15 p.m.

Iris watched Nora return to the table with her book. Upon closer inspection, Iris noticed it was a mystery novel by one of her favorite authors, Jonah James. After Nora sat down, Iris said, "That's the latest Jonah James mystery. What do you think of it?"

"It's been pretty good so far. This plot focuses on a rich older woman who suspects one of her heirs is trying to poison her, but nobody believes her. It's been very intriguing."

Iris nodded her head, saying, "That sounds good. I'll have to check it out. I've read his other books and really enjoyed them. How about you?" But before Nora could answer, the server returned with Iris's order.

A short while later, Nora got her food, and the two ate in silence. But once they got comfortable, Iris, her curiosity piqued, said, "So, Nora, what kind of job do you have? I'm quite curious to know."

Nora looked surprised as she said, "I'm a reporter for the *Orlando Print* newspaper. What about you?"

Iris's eyes widened as she asked, her voice barely a whisper, "Nora, could it be? Did you... work on the Underwood case ten years ago?"

Nora looked surprised as she said, "Yes, I did. I'm surprised you remember that, considering it happened so long ago."

"It was a big case back then. It became a topic of conversation everywhere, especially since it was never solved. But as for your earlier question, I was a stay-at-home parent for most of my life. My husband was the breadwinner for the family. I got lucky and stayed home and raised our two kids."

Nora's smile faded slightly as she said, her voice tinged with a hint of sadness, "That sounds nice but old-fashioned. I was more focused on my career, and I never had any kids of my own. Not that I didn't try."

Iris's eyebrow rose as she asked, "Oh, what happened?" Nora went to speak, but the server returned with their bill just then, and the conversation dropped.

After each of them charged their card to their cabin, the two women got up and went their separate ways. Iris headed back up to her room to call her son and update him on all the crazy things that had happened to her today.

17

Present Day
Friday, August 9, 2024, 7:15 p.m.

Iris stood outside her cabin. After unlocking the door, she entered before closing and locking the door. Then Iris headed to the bar in the kitchen and sat down. Once she got comfortable, she rang up her son. After several rings, Samuel picked up the phone and said, "Good evening, Mom. How has the cruise been so far?"

"It's been good for the most part. But you won't believe who I ran into today on the ship."

"Well, now I'm interested. Who did you run into?"

Iris couldn't contain her surprise as she exclaimed, "Charles Underwood and Nora Brooks, that news reporter who wrote those infamous articles about him ten years ago!"

Samuel uttered surprise as he said, "That's crazy. What are the odds those two would show up on the same cruise all these years later? Did seeing Charles Underwood onboard upset you? I know it might bring up some terrible memories."

"Initially, it bothered me, but since he was never convicted of any crimes, he has just as much right to be on this cruise as

I do. But seeing him brought back memories of your father working on the case. He was really bothered that he hadn't solved it."

"Did Dad not save his old case file at the house?"

"Yes, Sammy, he did. I still have it put up in my room from where your father had left it before he died. He had wanted to try working on it again once he retired but didn't get the chance. But I never expected I would run into Charles here again. Life can be strange at times."

"You're telling me, Mom. It's also odd that a reporter would be on board. Do you think she was following Charles or someone else?"

Iris pondered momentarily before saying, "I don't think so. But Charles approached her at dinner. Maybe he recognized her and was asking if she was tracking him. I'll have to ask her what he said later if I get the chance. Not that it matters. It's not my business."

Samuel laughed and said, "You're right. It's none of our business, but it is a strange coincidence. I hope nothing bad is going to happen. But enough about that. What do you have planned to do tomorrow?"

"I'm not sure. I got a brochure of things I can check out. I guess I should look at that later. I'll let you know what I end up doing tomorrow. But for now, I think I'm going to unwind and relax for a little bit. So, goodnight, Sammy. I love you."

Iris heard her son say, "Good night, Mom. Love you too," before hanging up the phone. She sat there for a moment, the silence of the cabin enveloping her. The events of the day replayed in her mind, and she couldn't help but wonder what tomorrow would bring.

18

Present Day
Friday, August 9, 2024, Night

Charles just entered his cabin after returning from dinner. Once inside, he spotted a handwritten note on the ground. Once he picked it up, he read the message written on it. It read,

"Hello, old friend. Meet me on the pool deck tonight for an old reunion."

How interesting, Charles thought. At the bottom of the page, instead of a signature, was a lipstick kiss. Charles felt intrigued. He wondered who sent the message. Perhaps it was… But just then, his phone rang, cutting off his thoughts. He noticed it was a business call, so he hit answer and got down to business.

With the business call behind him, Charles turned his attention back to the note. He remembered the complimentary bottle of champagne that was supposed to accompany his evening. Finding it on his nightstand, he popped the bottle and settled in, the anticipation of the upcoming reunion adding a spark to his evening. He was eager to meet his mysterious guest and see what the night held in store.

Stepping onto the pool deck, Charles found himself in a dimly lit space. He scanned the area, half-expecting to find it empty. But then, he heard footsteps behind him. Turning, he was met with a sight that left him speechless. The mystery guest, the sender of the note, stood before him.

"Good evening, Charles. I'm glad you decided to come," the guest greeted him.

Charles stood in shock as he said, "Good evening to you as well. I'm sorry for what happened in the past."

"Don't worry about it. Actually, I have something for us to toast to. The future."

Charles felt intrigued as he watched his guest pull out a bottle of scotch. After opening it, his guest handed the bottle to him and said, "Take a sip for old times' sake."

Charles hesitated momentarily but thought maybe he might get lucky if he did. So, he took a big gulp. His guest smiled in response, but the look creeped Charles out. A moment later, his vision faded to black. Something was wrong. He stumbled closer to his visitor for help but collapsed before he got the chance to.

19

Present Day
Saturday, August 10, 2024, 6:30 a.m.

Iris tossed and turned in bed, trying to fall back asleep to no avail. Thoughts of Charles Underwood kept popping up in her head. Scenes of her departed husband coming home, upset about the lack of progress in the case, also came to mind. Iris sighed in defeat, realizing she wouldn't get any rest any time soon. So, she threw the covers off her body and got out of bed.

Iris went to the kitchen to start a pot of coffee. While it was brewing, she reviewed the ship's itinerary for the day. The only thing that caught her eye was a trivia night contest that was supposed to be held at the bar on the pool deck. She might have to check that out later. But the thought of taking a morning swim sounded appealing to Iris, so she changed into her swimsuit and grabbed a towel. After she finished, she went and checked on the coffee. It was done. After making a small to-go cup, she headed out the door and towards deck nine.

As Iris approached the pool, disbelief came across her face. She dropped her coffee cup and heard it shatter on the floor as she screamed. Lying face down in the pool was the body of Charles Underwood.

A few moments later, a cruise employee approached Iris from the stairwell to inquire about what was going on. Iris pointed to the pool, and the employee quickly glanced at it. Shock covered their face as they exclaimed, "Oh no! What happened?"

Iris murmured, "I came up here for a morning swim and found him dead in the pool. And I dropped my coffee cup and broke it. My bad."

The employee said, "I see. I need to go get help and a broom and dustpan so that I can clean up this mess. Can you watch the pool and make sure nothing is disturbed until then?"

Iris said, "Sure thing," before the worker rushed off to find help.

As Iris waited for help to arrive, she slowly felt trapped in one of her cozy mystery stories. She knew she probably shouldn't try to play detective, but it was an odd coincidence that Charles would drown on the first night of the cruise right after he went and talked to Nora. Plus, if her husband were here, he would have tried to see if anything strange had happened. So, she convinced herself that it wouldn't hurt to examine the crime scene to see if anything stood out as odd to her.

Iris scanned the pool for clues. It still looked pristine despite the dead body of Charles Underwood floating in it. From the look of things, he was still wearing the same outfit he had worn at dinner. But if he had come up here to swim after dinner, surely there were people here to help if he was drowning. So, the only logical thing was that he died late at night. But if that was the case, why did he come up here so late by himself? Unless he wanted a late-night swim, Iris guessed. But that didn't feel right to her. As she paced back and forth, something at the bottom of the pool caught her eye. She wondered if it was a clue when she heard footsteps. She turned around and saw the cruise employee return carrying a broom, dustpan, and a man in a sailor's uniform.

20

Present Day
Saturday, August 10, 2024, 7:00 a.m.

As Iris stepped into the ship's lounge, she noticed the man in a sailor uniform's name tag, which read Captain Rivers. While he introduced himself, his employee worked diligently to clean up the broken coffee cup.

The captain said, "I'm sorry you had to see that, Miss. However, I need you to tell me what happened."

After Iris told the captain what she had seen, she said, "While I was waiting for you to arrive, I thought I saw something at the bottom of the pool."

"Where did you spot it?" asked the captain.

Iris pointed to the spot in the pool. The captain looked over and told his worker to fetch something to pull it out. The worker ran off, leaving the two alone. The two stood in awkward silence. A few moments later, the worker returned with a long net and quickly retrieved the sunken object. The captain went over to see what it was. After a moment, he said, "It's a bottle of scotch. Most likely from the minibar in his room. But we'll have to check. It seems like the man got drunk last night and tried to go swimming. It's such a shame. However, we won't know for sure until the ship's doctor performs an autopsy."

Iris's mind was racing, her thoughts a jumble of confusion and doubt. The captain's deduction seemed plausible, but something didn't quite add up. As the captain told his worker to fetch the ship's doctor, Iris's unease grew. Once the employee ran off again, the captain turned, his gaze steady but his voice tinged with regret, and said, "I'm sorry you had to deal with this. But I would like to ask you to leave for now until we can get the body out of the pool. This floor is going to be unavailable until we get everything cleaned up. But it should be open again later if you wish to return."

Iris replied, "I understand, captain," her voice barely above a whisper before she left the scene and returned to her room. Her mind was filled with questions and a growing sense of unease.

21

Present Day
Saturday, August 10, 2024, 7:30 a.m.

Iris was sitting at the bar in her room with her phone in her hand. She impatiently tapped her fingers on the counter while waiting for the Wi-Fi to load. One inconvenience of being out at sea was the lack of a stable internet connection. After a few more minutes of nothing loading, Iris threw her hands up in defeat. Maybe she would have better luck on a higher floor of the ship. But just then, her stomach growled, reminding her she still hadn't eaten breakfast. She attributed it to the stress of finding Charles Underwood's body in the pool. Iris still couldn't believe he was dead. Despite not being a fan of his, she still felt upset at the loss of life. Since the Wi-Fi wasn't working, Iris guessed her research would have to wait. Plus, she needed to get something to eat. She recalled seeing some cozy cafes being located somewhere. But she couldn't remember where. She thought that maybe there was a map in the itinerary the stewardess had left. So, she went to grab it.

After locating it, Iris flipped through the pages until she

found what she was looking for. According to the map, the cafes were on deck seven. With her destination in mind, Iris went and got her purse out of the bedroom. After retrieving it, she placed the brochure inside. Then, made her way to deck seven for breakfast.

IRIS SCANNED DECK SEVEN, TAKING IN THE FLOOR'S LAYOUT. The middle of the room housed the ship's library, a haven of knowledge and intrigue. From the outside, it looked more like a bookstore to her, with its giant glass panels showing off rows of books, each a potential clue in the mystery she was unraveling. But regardless of that, she still planned on going there later and checking it out. Next to the library were cafes on both sides, their warm lights and inviting aromas promising a respite from the cold reality of the ship's mysteries. There were three cafes on each side of the library. But despite having six options, they all looked the same to Iris, who hadn't been to a cafe before. So, she chose one at random and made her way inside.

Upon entering the cafe, Iris immediately smelled the aroma of fresh coffee and homemade pastries. The smell made her stomach growl as she checked out the cafe. The inside of the cafe was cozy, with various coffee-related paintings and signs hanging in strategic areas. Scattered around the room were several bistro tables with matching chairs. Finishing the look was a counter that displayed a glass box that showed off the freshly made pastries, and above the counter was a whiteboard with a handwritten menu. Iris nodded in approval as she walked over to the counter and gave her order. While waiting for her food, she scanned the cafe to see who was around. And then, Nora walked into the cafe. A light bulb came on. Iris needed to talk to her about Charles's death to see how she would react. So, after receiving her order, Iris sat at one table, waiting for Nora to get her order.

A few minutes later, Nora got her food and headed to a

table. Iris waited for her to sit down before going over and saying, "Good morning, Nora. I hope I'm not disturbing you, but something crazy happened this morning that I thought you should know."

Nora looked up in surprise and said, "Good morning to you as well. What's the crazy thing you wanted to tell me?"

Iris casually said, "I found Charles Underwood dead in the pool this morning." Nora's eyes widened in shock, her face pale as she struggled to process the news. Iris waited patiently, her heart pounding in her chest, for Nora's response, her mind racing with the possibilities of what this revelation could mean for their journey.

22

Ten Years Ago
Friday, July 11, 2014, Evening

Nora struggled to move as she forced herself to walk to the shower. After some effort, she removed her clothing. As she entered the shower, Nora winced in pain as she looked at the bruises on her arms and legs as she turned on the water. Tears ran down her face as she remembered how Charles had hit her. All because she spilled her wine on his shirt. Nora knew she should report the abuse. But the words Charles had threatened her with still rang in her ears.

"If you try to go to the police, I'll kill you and your precious baby sister." The thought of losing her sister was too much to bear, so Nora didn't contact the police. But as the water fell across her body, she made a promise to herself. If Charles hit her again, she was going to be the one doing the killing instead of him.

23

Present Day
Saturday, August 10, 2024, 7:50 a.m.

Iris watched Nora turn pale as she said, "That's horrible. Do you think it was an accident? That he drowned?"

It was a good question, Iris thought as she said, "That seems to be the case. I found him face down in the pool. It was quite a shock, for sure. But they still need to perform an autopsy to confirm."

Nora's hands shook as she reached for her bag and pulled out a prescription bottle. After retrieving two pills, she placed them in her mouth before taking a drink of her coffee and swallowing. Then she said, "Sorry about that. My anxiety was acting up over that horrible tale. So, I wanted to take my pills. That must have been a terrible way to die."

Iris thought the same thing. Drowning had to be a horrid way to die. She couldn't believe Charles had gotten drunk and tried swimming so late at night alone. Something about it didn't align with his image as a successful business tycoon. Plus, there was the matter of Nora knowing Charles Underwood and how he had confronted her yesterday at dinner. It made Iris wonder if there was some connection to his death. So, she said, "It's odd how he drowned last night after having confronted you at dinner. Since you worked on the Underwood case all those years ago, what was it he was talking to you about?"

Nora looked angry, saying, "Why is it odd that I wrote about the Underwood case ten years ago? I had just started working as a reporter, and it was a big case then. As for last night, Charles was merely trying to flirt with me. I doubt if he even recognized who I was. Besides, what business is it of yours?"

Iris considered this information momentarily before saying, "That makes sense. I'm sorry if I appeared rude. My late husband was the police officer in charge of the Underwood case, and he always suspected Charles was connected to his wife's disappearance and his administrative assistant's death but could never prove it. When I found Charles dead, I wondered if his death had any connection to what had happened in the past."

Nora grew more upset as she said, "You're wrong. That happened a long time ago and couldn't possibly be connected to his death." Then she grabbed her food and got up before continuing, "If you'll excuse me, I have things to do," before taking off.

Iris sat in surprise as she watched Nora storm off. That certainly struck a nerve, she thought. But the question was why. Iris mused as she continued to eat her breakfast. She thought some research was in order, but first, she needed to finish breakfast. So, Iris sat in thought as she finished eating her breakfast and planned her next move.

24

Present Day
Saturday, August 10, 2024, 8:10 a.m.

Sandy walked forward as the elevator doors opened, his face buried in his phone. While doing so, he bumped into someone, and both fell to the ground. As they stood, Sandy said, "I'm so sorry, I wasn't paying attention. Are you okay?"

Upon closer inspection, he saw it was Nora as she said, "I'm fine. But that's why you shouldn't look at your phone while walking."

Sandy, his cheeks tinged with red, mustered a smile. "You're right. I should be more careful. Can I make it up to you?" he asked, his voice filled with genuine concern.

Nora, her voice tinged with annoyance, broke the silence, "Just be more mindful of your surroundings. I have things to attend to, so take care," before briskly walking towards the elevator.

Sandy, feeling a pang of disappointment, watched Nora disappear into the elevator. His attempt to start a conversation had backfired, leaving him with a sense of regret. Determined to make amends, he resolved to find another opportunity to connect with her as he made his way to breakfast.

25

Present Day
Saturday, August 10, 2024, 8:30 a.m.

Selina watched as Jordan ran eagerly up the steps to the door of deck nine in his swimsuit. She admired the view as she followed behind him. But once he arrived at the door, he stopped, causing her to stop abruptly so she wouldn't run into him. She wondered what the matter was as he said, "The door is locked! There is a sign on the door saying there was some accident and they had to close the floor temporarily. I wonder what's going on?"

"I wonder what happened. Is there any information about when it will be open again?" Selina asked, her voice filled with concern.

"It doesn't give an exact time. The sign indicates that they will announce when the floor is open again," Jordan said, his voice tinged with disappointment.

"Well, that's unfortunate. But there is nothing we can do about it for the moment. I guess we should go change our clothes."

"Sounds good to me. Afterward, I'm really looking forward to getting some breakfast," Jordan said, his stomach rumbling in agreement.

Selina smiled and said, "That sounds good to me," before turning around and heading back to their cabin.

26

Present Day
Saturday, August 10, 2024, 9:00 a.m.

Georgia settled into a cozy corner of the cafe, her green tea latte warming her hands. She couldn't help but smile as she observed Tyler, his charm in full swing at the checkout line. Moments later, he joined her at the table, his face betraying a hint of shyness. Georgia couldn't resist teasing him, "So, did you get his number?"

Tyler blushed as he said, "Maybe," while taking a bite out of his blueberry muffin.

Georgia laughed, saying, "Good for you, sugar. He is cute."

Tyler beamed as he said, "I know, right? He even gave me a discount on my food."

Georgia laughed, saying, "I should've ordered after you. Then maybe your new boyfriend would have also given me a discount."

"He's not my boyfriend. At least not yet," said Tyler.

"I know, sweetie. I was teasing…" But before she could continue, the intercom came on.

"Good morning, everyone. This is Captain Rivers speaking. I just wanted to announce that deck nine will be temporarily closed today. An accident occurred last night, and some maintenance work needs to be done. But the pool, bar, and lounge should be accessible by noon. So, for those interested in using these facilities, they will be open then. However, for safety reasons, starting tonight after 10 p.m., the doors to this floor will be locked. Apart from that, I hope everyone has a great day on the SS Paradise."

Tyler's eyes sparkled with curiosity as he mused, "I wonder what could have happened there last night?"

"I don't know," Georgia began as she took a sip of her drink before she continued, "Maybe someone went there last night and got hurt or something."

Tyler took a bite of his muffin before saying, "Perhaps you're right. Or maybe someone tried to vandalize the place. Guess the only way to know for sure is to go there later and look around."

"That sounds like a good idea to me, sweetheart. But they said it wouldn't be open again until 1 p.m., so we have some time to kill."

Tyler finished his muffin, his eyes twinkling mischievously. "So, what's the plan, girlfriend? How should we kill time until then?"

Georgia pondered this question momentarily before saying, "I guess we could try exploring to see if anything strikes our fancy."

"Sounds good to me. I'm ready to go whenever you are."

"Okay, I am too." Then, the two got up from the table, threw away their trash, and left the cafe.

27

Present Day
Saturday, August 10, 2024, 9:15 a.m.

Iris sat frustrated on the sofa in her cabin, trying to get the Wi-Fi to work. But, like earlier, it was acting incredibly slow. She wanted to research Charles Underwood and his current connection to Nora. But at that moment, that didn't seem like it would happen. "This is ridiculous," she muttered to herself. But just then, a thought occurred to her. The ship had a library, meaning they might have computers connected to their own Wi-Fi. If she was lucky, then maybe she could do her research there. But Iris sighed when she realized she had just left the deck where the library was located earlier today. "Of course, it's never that easy," she grumbled. Sounds about right, Iris thought as she got up from the sofa. After retrieving her purse, she headed toward the library.

As Iris entered the library, the smell of new books hit her nose. The smell brought a smile to her face. She glanced around and saw rows and rows of bookshelves scattered all around the room but no computers. The sight brought a frown to her face. Where could they be? She wondered. So,

Iris walked past the row of books in search of her prize, her footsteps echoing softly in the quiet room. Sure enough, a row of computers was in the back of the room. "There they are," she whispered, a hint of triumph in her voice, as she went and took an empty seat.

The computer was working much faster than Iris's phone was back in her room, but it was still slower than she was used to back home. It reminded her of when she first got a home computer, and dial-up internet was the big thing. She thought about how things had changed since then as she opened a *Google* search engine and typed in Charles Underwood's name.

As she scanned through the new articles, Iris noticed something interesting. Besides the ones that talked about the tenth anniversary of his wife Stacy's disappearance, most of the articles dated back several years. That led her to believe that if anything fishy was connected to Charles's death, then it was likely because the old case was brought back up because of the anniversary. Switching gears, she searched for recent articles mentioning Nora's name. A quick search showed that Nora had written articles about Charles, accusing him of many awful things ranging from cheating to embezzlement. However, as the article had stated, they never proved anything. But those articles date back almost ten years ago. So, Iris questioned how they could connect those articles to Charles. But it made her wonder if he had recognized Nora at dinner and confronted her all these years later or if he was merely trying to hit on her, as she had put it. For now, there was no way of telling. Iris thought she learned all she could for now and closed her search browser before getting up. She thought her next move would be to call her son and see if he could email her the old case files of her late husband. So, with that in mind, she headed back to her room.

28

Present Day
Saturday, August 10, 2024, 10:30 a.m.

Iris sat comfortably on the sofa as she rang up her son. After a few rings, he answered, "Good morning, Mom. I only got a few minutes. What do you need?"

"Sorry to bother you," Iris began, "But something crazy happened this morning. I had trouble sleeping, so I went for a morning swim. But when I got to the pool, I found Charles Underwood face down in the pool, dead. It was quite a shock, I tell you."

"I can't believe it! I'm glad you're all right. Do you think it was an accident or something else?"

"Well, when the captain came and got the body out of the pool, I noticed something at the bottom of the pool, so I pointed it out. When they fished it out, they found an empty bottle of scotch. It seems like maybe he got drunk and maybe tried to go swimming late at night. But my gut tells me there is more to it than that. Plus, I saw Charles scream at Nora last night at dinner. This seems like a strange coincidence."

"You're right. That seems odd. But it proves nothing.

Maybe he got drunk and drowned. But as you said, Mom, I think there might be more to the story. Without proof, what can you do?"

"I see what you're getting at. But if someone killed Charles somehow, then that means there is a killer onboard the cruise ship, and I can't feel safe until the killer is caught."

"I get what you're saying, Mom, but I cannot actively help you hunt a killer. If you were to get hurt, I wouldn't be able to forgive myself."

Iris sighed with frustration as she said, "I understand that. But if you don't, I'll ask Stel to do it instead. It might not seem very smart, but if your father were alive, he would try to investigate this matter until its end. As you know, the Underwood case was one of the few cases your dad never solved. So, I feel obligated to solve Charles's death. Whether that leads us to discover that Charles died from an unfortunate accident or if someone murdered him."

Samuel sighed loudly as he said, "All right, you win, Mom. I'll go to your house later and do it. But you will need to tell me where the case files are located."

After Iris told her son where the papers were, she said, "Thanks, Sammy. It means a lot. I know you are busy, so I'll let you go. Goodbye, love." She heard her son saying goodbye before hanging up. Then she checked the time. It was still a while before the pool would be open again, so she had some time to kill. Suddenly, her eyes felt heavy. Iris thought a nap was in order. So, after setting an alarm for 1 p.m., she went to lie down for a while.

29

Ten Years Ago
Saturday, August 23, 2014, Evening

Iris placed the chicken into a shake-and-bake ziplock bag, and the sound of the chicken hitting the bag echoed in the kitchen. After sealing it, she shook the bag up and down, feeling the weight of the chicken shifting inside. Once satisfied, Iris opened the bag and placed the chicken on a cooking sheet, the cold metal of the sheet chilling her fingertips. After she finished, she preheated the oven to 375, and the warm air from the oven filled the kitchen. While waiting for the oven to heat, she turned on the TV, the sound of the talk show host's voice filling the room.

The Larry King show popped up on the screen. Iris noticed the headline *Interview with Real Estate Tycoon Charles Underwood, Bereaved Husband,* displayed at the bottom of the screen. How interesting, Iris thought as she listened to the interview. Larry was asking Charles some basic questions about his life. Most of the information was old news, but she learned that Stacy Underwood had met Charles in high school and married shortly after graduating. Iris also learned that Stacy went to college for journalism while Charles went for his business degree and real estate license. After graduating, Stacy worked for the *Orlando Gazette* as a reporter while Charles interned as a real estate agent. Shortly after, he started his own real estate business. Larry talked more about the case when she heard a ding signaling that the oven was preheated.

As Iris turned off the TV, she carefully placed the cooking tray into the oven, setting the timer on the stove for twenty minutes. Her ears perked up at the sound of the front door opening, and a warm smile spread across her face, her heart fluttering at the thought of her husband's imminent arrival.

A few moments later, Henry entered the kitchen, his tired eyes lighting up at the sight of his wife. Iris, too, couldn't hide her joy, a smile spreading across her face. But she quickly stepped back, concern replacing her smile as she said, "You need a shower. Did you have a tough day at work?"

Henry laughed, his voice filled with exhaustion, saying, "Sorry, I've been running around like a chicken with its head cut off. This Underwood case is going to be the death of me."

"Oh, I hope not. I still need you to pay the bills," Iris playfully teased, a twinkle in her eye.

Henry laughed as he said, "Don't worry, dear, your meal ticket isn't going anywhere any time soon."

Iris kissed him before saying, "I'm just kidding, love. But you need to take a bath."

"I know I'll go take one in a second. But first, I want to know what's for dinner?"

"Shake and bake chicken."

Henry licked his lips before saying, "Sounds delicious." Then he winked before continuing, "Almost as good as you."

Iris laughed as she said, "Yeah, right, Romeo. Go take your bath."

With a mischievous smile, Henry said, "Okay, but if you want to join me, I wouldn't complain."

Iris laughed as she looked at the timer on the stove. The time read ten minutes. She thought there wasn't enough time and said, "Sorry, love, but the chicken is almost done, and I don't want to burn it."

Henry gave a mock frown as he said, "Okay, dear. Maybe we can have dessert after dinner, then?"

Iris laughed as she said, "Maybe if you behave yourself. Now go and take your shower."

Henry chuckled as he said, "Yes, ma'am," before he took off towards the shower.

30

Present Day
Saturday, August 10, 2024, 1:00 p.m.

Iris stood in a hallway, looking through a two-way mirror. On the other side of the mirror, Iris watched a shadowy figure push a drunken Charles into the pool and drown. Afterward, the shadowy figure laughed maliciously before disappearing into the night. The sight brought horror to Iris's face as she heard her alarm go off. Iris jumped up in her bed at the sound of it going off, and her eyes opened. What a scary dream, she thought as she reached over and turned off her alarm. After stretching, Iris got out of bed and got ready to go to the pool.

As Iris approached the pool, she noticed a couple glancing around the pool curiously. She guessed they were speculating about what had happened. Iris debated whether she should go over there and tell them what she had found. After a few moments, she walked over to see if she could overhear their conversation. As Iris approached the couple, she heard the woman say, "As far as I can tell, nothing looks different from yesterday. It makes you wonder what happened?"

The man beside her replied, "Perhaps it was mild vandalism that was easy to clean up."

"Maybe," the woman began, "Or perhaps someone drowned in the pool."

That comment piqued her interest. Perhaps she should talk to the couple and see if they knew more, especially that woman. It couldn't hurt, Iris thought. So, she approached the couple.

"Excuse me," began Iris, "But I overheard you guys discussing why the pool was closed earlier. I can tell you what happened if you're interested."

The couple looked intrigued as the man said, "Oh really? Please spill the tea, girlfriend. What happened?"

"Well, I discovered a man face down in the pool this morning."

Shock covered the couple's faces as the woman said, "That's horrible. Do you think it was some accident?"

"It might have been. He was found with an empty bottle of alcohol in his clothes when they fished him out of the pool."

"That's such a dumb thing to do," the man said, "Getting drunk and trying to go swimming alone at night. What must he have been thinking? Do you have any idea who it was?"

Iris was curious to see their reaction as she said, "Yes, I do. The man's name was Charles Underwood." The couple turned to each other, surprised, as an awkward silence hung in the air.

31

Ten Years Ago
Saturday, May 17, 2014, Evening

Charles pulled into the dimly lit parking lot. After parking his car in the back, he made his way to the discreet side entrance of the strip club. Once there, he scanned his membership card before entering.

Inside, an usher escorted Charles back to a private viewing room. A few moments later, a server came in and handed Charles his usual drink.

"How long until Cherry shows up for my dance?" Charles asked, tipping the man.

The server replied nervously, "I'm sorry, sir, but Cherry is out tonight. But if you would allow me to offer a suggestion, Peaches is a new dancer you might be interested in. She has long, slender legs, golden skin, and fiery red hair."

Charles licked his lips in excitement as he said, "I think she will work nicely. When will she be ready?"

"A few minutes, sir. Let me go get her."

Charles waved a hand as he said, "Go on, boy. Don't keep me waiting."

The server mumbled, "Yes, sir," before hurrying off.

A few minutes later, a young woman appeared in a skimpy peach outfit. As the server had said, the woman matched his description. Charles liked what he saw very much.

As Peaches approached him, she said, "What would you like me to do, sir?"

Charles said hungrily, "I want a lap dance."

Peaches replied, "Yes, sir," before getting to work.

After Peaches had finished her dance, she said, "That will be fifty bucks."

As Charles reached for his wallet, a primal urge coursed through him. His face was flush from the dance he had just received. Charles felt the need to take this girl home with him for the night. So, after paying Peaches, he said in an eager tone, "How much would it cost for you to come and join me for the night?"

"Depends on how well you perform," said Peaches with a wink.

Charles laughed at this girl's spunk, saying, "Well, I don't think you'll be too disappointed."

The girl laughed before replying, "I'm intrigued, handsome. But before we leave, I'll have to inform my boss."

"That's fine, but don't keep me waiting too long."

Peaches winked as she said, "Don't worry; I won't," before taking off to look for her boss. A few minutes later, she returned and gave Charles the thumbs-up to leave. Then, he led her outside the club towards his car.

WHEN CHARLES WOKE UP THE NEXT DAY, THE GIRL WAS missing. The image made him a little sad. Charles had enjoyed his time with her last night and knew he would have to see her again when his wife was out of town. Speaking of his wife, when was she supposed to return home today? Charles couldn't remember, so he went to grab his phone off the side table by his bed. But while doing so, he found a handwritten note. It must be from that girl from last night, he reasoned as he read the message.

Dear handsome,

Last night was a lot of fun. If you're ever interested in another round, please request Peaches at Long Legs. I usually work Fridays to Tuesdays from 6:00 p.m. to 4:00 a.m. But regardless, I quite enjoyed myself and hope to see you again.

P.S. If I see you again, please call me Georgia.

Charles laughed as he put the note away. He was glad that she had enjoyed herself. He smiled as he opened his phone and checked when his wife would be home. Her text said 11 a.m. Charles checked the time. The clock read 9:45 a.m. She would be here soon, and he needed to clean up the room before she returned. He sighed as he got out of bed and got to work.

32

Ten Years Ago
Friday, May 30, 2014, Evening

Tyler was back at his workstation getting all his supplies set up for the night when he heard someone enter the room. He hoped it was Georgia. A smile came to his face as he turned around to see. He was pleasantly surprised to see it was Georgia. She was carrying her usual outfit, a skimpy peach costume. But she was moving in a hurry. No doubt she was running out of time before her first performance. Georgia glanced at Tyler as she approached the curtain that served as a makeshift changing room and said, "Sorry, Ty, I'm running behind. I'll be ready in a minute."

Tyler smiled as he said, "No problem, girlfriend," as he watched her enter the changing room.

A few minutes passed before Georgia exited and joined Tyler at his makeup station. Tyler got to work putting on her makeup. As he was doing so, Georgia said, "Sorry for making you rush tonight. I was hanging out with that hunk that picked me up a few weeks ago and lost track of time."

Tyler laughed as he said, "No worries, dear. He is a fine-looking man for his age."

This caused Georgia to laugh as she said, "True, he might be a tad older than your boyfriend, Ryan, but age can bring a degree of charm as well."

"I agree. A little gray in your hair can make a man look wise and distinguished, and that guy you have been hanging out with surely looks the part. What is his name again?"

Georgia blushed as she said, "Charles."

"That's got a nice ring to it."

Georgia smiled as she replied, "I know, right..." But before she could continue, the manager came in and said that it was ten minutes until show time. Georgia said, "Guess we need to wrap this up then."

"No worries, we're almost done here." A few moments later, he had finished and said, "There you go, GG. Knock them dead."

Georgia smiled as she said, "Thanks," before taking off to start her shift.

33

Present Day
Saturday, August 10, 2024, 1:20 p.m.

Iris watched as the couple stood in shock at her statement that she had found Charles dead in the pool. After the couple had a few moments to gather their thoughts, the woman said, "What are the odds that it was him who died?"

The man jumped in and said, "Serves him right. He was wicked, and it sounds like he received his karma."

"Is that because of what happened to his wife or something else?" asked Iris.

The man took a moment to reply before saying, "That too, but I was talking about…" before he stopped halfway through his comment.

How strange, Iris thought as she said, "Well, what were you referring to then, mister? I'm sorry, but what are your guys' names?"

The couple laughed as the man said, "That's right, we never introduced ourselves. My name is Tyler Reed. And my friend here is Georgia Fisher. But as for your other question, I don't think I'm at liberty to discuss that since it involves my friend."

"I guess I should fill you in. I'm assuming Tyler is referring to the fact that Charles and I had a falling out a long time ago. But that was years ago, and I haven't spoken to him since then. It's a terrible business of him drowning, though."

Iris thought the statement made sense, but she wasn't sure if it was the complete truth, as she said, "I see. I'm sorry to hear that."

Georgia laughed and said, "You're all good, honey. But Tyler and I have some things to do, so take care, Mrs. ..." Georgia paused momentarily before continuing, "I'm sorry, but what is your name, dear?"

"My name is Iris May."

Both said it was nice to meet her before taking off. As she considered her next move, Iris wondered if there was more to their story. After a few moments, Iris thought a drink sounded good, so she headed to the bar to get something.

34

Present Day
Saturday, August 10, 2024, 1:45 p.m.

As Iris approached the bar, she noticed a handsome young man sipping a beer at one end of the bar. Iris bet the man had many admirers as she took a seat at the bar. A few minutes later, the bartender arrived and took her order. Iris debated on asking the bartender what had happened earlier at the pool to see what the staff was told to say about the incident. Ultimately, she decided it wouldn't hurt to ask. So, once the bartender returned with her drink, Iris paid the man and said, "Thanks for the drink. If it's all right to ask, do you know why the pool was closed earlier?"

The bartender smiled reassuringly as he said, "Nothing too serious, just some unexpected maintenance to the pool, that's all."

Iris thought it made sense that the cruise didn't want to advertise that a man had drowned in the pool. Might cause a panic, she thought. But she wanted to dig deeper and said, "That's good to hear. I had heard a rumor that a well-to-do man had drowned."

The bartender turned pale as he said, "Well, nothing of the sort happened. I wonder how someone got that idea."

Iris blushed, saying, "I guess they just got a wild imagination then."

The bartender laughed awkwardly, saying, "I guess so. I got to go serve other clients if you need me, just holler," before taking off to another customer on the other side of the bar. Iris found the interaction interesting. She wondered if the captain would pay her a visit later, reminding her to be discreet about the matter. But just then, her thoughts got interrupted by the sound of someone sitting down beside her.

Upon closer inspection, Iris realized it was the handsome young man she had admired earlier. She wondered why he had moved when she heard him say, "Sorry to disturb you, Miss, but I thought I overheard you talking to the bartender about a possible wealthy man who has drowned in the pool. I was wondering who told you that story?"

Iris contemplated whether to tell this man the truth. What if he was involved in Charles's death? Iris knew it was silly to think such nonsense. As far as she knew, Charles had drowned because of negligence on his part. So, it couldn't possibly hurt to say anything, so Iris said, "Well, actually, I found the man in the pool this morning when I was going to go for a morning swim. He was face down in the pool. I was asking the bartender because I was curious what the captain told the workers to say if anyone asked about it."

"That's crazy," began the man before continuing, "but it makes sense. They don't want to cause an uproar or something. Do you know who the man was?"

Iris looked carefully at the man and said, "I do. His name is Charles Underwood."

The man looked wide-eyed and stared at Iris momentarily as if in a daze.

35

A Week Ago
Friday, August 3, 2024, Afternoon

Sandy was sitting at his desk, sifting through papers, when he heard his front door open. As he turned to look up, he saw a man with short, curly hair carrying a manila folder. Sandy, being the professional that he was, said, "Hello there, what can I do for you?"

The man eagerly said, "I was wondering if you work on missing person cases."

Sandy expressed intrigue, saying, "Yes, I do. Who is it you want me to locate?"

The man's voice quivered slightly as he spoke, "It might be unconventional, but I need you to find my wife, Stacy. She vanished without a trace ten years ago." He patted the folder in his hands, adding, "This file contains information that might help you in your search."

Sandy felt a mix of sympathy and uncertainty as he said, "I see. I can try my best to find your missing wife, but since it's been ten years, I'm not sure how helpful I can be. This is quite a challenging case."

The man shook his head, saying, "I understand that, sir. But I got a tip from a source that says that this reporter named Nora Brooks knows something about my wife's current whereabouts. So, I wanted you to see if you could follow her and determine if this information is true."

Sandy felt like this would be a wild goose chase when he asked, "Can I ask who this source is that gave you this tip?"

"Sorry, but that's confidential. I can assure you that it is a credible source."

Sandy thought as much as he said, "I see. If I were to take on the case, it would be an upfront fee of $250 and an investigation fee that I would charge up to $1500 for expenses. Does that work for you?"

"Yes, that works for me. I can pay right now if that pleases you."

Sandy felt like taking candy from a baby but also needed the money, so he said, "Sure, that works. Let me fill out a form for you to sign, and then you can pay."

"That sounds good to me."

Sandy pulled out a form from his desk and filled it out. Once satisfied, he handed it to his client to go over. The man signed eagerly before giving Sandy cash and heading out. After he left, Sandy realized he hadn't gotten his client's name. So, he looked down at the signed form and saw that the name read Charles Underwood. Sandy's mouth fell open, and he mentally kicked himself. If he had known who his client was, he could have charged more for his services. But Sandy knew that was extortion, and odds were this case wouldn't be much work, so he shouldn't complain. But it made him wonder who gave Charles a tip about this Nora woman and how Nora could possibly know where his missing wife was ten years later. That part intrigued him. Maybe this case wouldn't be so boring after all, Sandy thought as he opened the file and got to work, feeling a surge of anticipation for the investigation ahead.

36

Present Day
Saturday, August 10, 2024, 1:45 p.m.

Iris watched the man stare in shock as he said, "I'm sorry, but can you repeat that name again? I thought I heard you say Charles Underwood."

"You heard me right. The man who drowned was Charles Underwood. Do you know him somehow?"

The man looked uncertain for a moment before he said, "Nope. I never met the man, although I heard of him years ago when his wife disappeared."

Iris felt like he was lying about not knowing Charles but couldn't prove it, so she said, "Yes, it was a famous case ten years ago. I'm not surprised you recognized his name. It's crazy that he drowned on such a luxurious cruise like this."

The man seemed distracted as he said, "Yeah, it is. At least he can join his wife now."

That was one way to view it, she supposed. However, before she could say anything, the man said, "Sorry, but I just remembered I was supposed to meet somebody for lunch," before getting up and leaving. She wondered what was going on beneath that man's facade as she finished her drink. After she finished, Iris thought now would be a good time to explore the upper part of the ship, so she got up from the bar and made her way to deck ten.

Iris scanned the amenities on deck ten. From the sight of things, this floor was full of comfort sources, from its hair salon to its spa and wrapping up with its personal gym. She was sure that this floor was a popular spot on the ship. Not that she could blame them. Iris was interested in trying out all the services at some point. Since it would probably involve an appointment, Iris went inside and made them before checking out the gym.

The gym had its typical workout equipment, including various sets of weights, a few treadmills, a couple of benches, and some stationary bikes scattered around the room. Iris spotted an attractive young couple running on adjacent treadmills wearing matching workout clothes.

Seeing them working out together made her smile, so she walked to a stationary bike. After getting on, she pedaled at a low speed. As she pedaled, she overheard the couple talking about the accident at the pool, which piqued her interest. Iris heard the man say, "I still don't understand why they closed the pool, babe. There didn't seem to be anything the matter."

The woman replied, "I know. It makes you wonder if something shady happened, doesn't it?"

Iris wondered if she should go over there and talk to the couple. She quickly reasoned that if her husband had been here, he would have. So, Iris got off the bike, walked over to the couple, and said, "Sorry to interfere, but I heard you talking about why the pool was closed. I know what happened if you're interested."

This caught both of their attention when the woman said, "Yes, we are curious. Why was the pool closed?"

Iris watched in eager anticipation as she said, "A man named Charles Underwood was found face down in the pool dead." A look of dread covered both of their faces as Iris eagerly awaited a response.

37

Ten Years Ago
Friday, August 8, 2014, Night

Inga sat at her desk, the cool surface providing some relief from the heat of the room. She flipped through various invoices, the sound of paper rustling filling the air. Sweat ran down her face in thick drops as she went through each one for a fifth time. Despite hours of going through the invoices, Inga couldn't get the accounting books to balance. She was on the verge of tears when her work phone rang. She tried to regain her composure as she answered the phone, "*Underwood Real Estate*, Inga speaking, how may I help you?"

On the other end of the phone, she heard her boss say, "Inga, this is Charles. I want to know why the accounting books aren't on my desk yet. It's almost closing time for the weekend, and I'm about to head out soon."

Inga gulped as she said, "Sorry, sir, but no matter how many times I've tried to balance the books, I can't seem to balance them. Are you sure that there isn't anything missing?" She couldn't help but feel a pang of self-doubt. Was she not good enough for this job? Was she missing something obvious?

Charles' voice boomed through the phone, "YES, I'M SURE NONE ARE MISSING," but after a moment, he softened, "I'm sorry for yelling, but it's been a stressful day. Can you please come to my office with the invoices and accounting books? I'll try to see if we can figure out a solution."

Inga muttered, "Yes sir," before hearing Charles hang up the phone.

A few moments later, Inga stood outside her boss's door. After drawing a quick breath, she knocked firmly on the door. After a moment, she heard, "Come on in," before opening the door and stepping into Charles's office, a space that always seemed to be in a state of controlled chaos.

Once inside, Charles motioned Inga to sit down. So, she sat down in the slightly uncomfortable chair across from her boss. Once seated, Charles asked, "Thanks for coming so soon. Can I see the books and invoices so I can quickly review them?"

Inga said, "Sure thing," before getting up and handing her boss the requested items. After sitting back down, Inga watched her boss go through the invoices.

A short while later, Charles said, "I think you're right. It seems that there are some missing invoices. Let me see if I can find them in my desk drawer." He opened his desk and flipped through various files. A few moments later, he laid out a few forms on his desk and said, "Here are the missing forms. I'm sorry for causing you any stress, Inga. Can you add these to the accounting books before heading home?"

Frustrated but ready to leave, Inga said, "Sure thing, boss." Before getting up and grabbing the papers.

But as she turned around to leave the room, Charles said, "Thanks for understanding, Inga. You can leave the books on your desk, and I'll grab them on my way out."

Inga replied, "No problem, sir," before returning to her office.

Once inside her office, Inga glanced at the missing

invoices. She smiled as she added up the amounts and saw they equaled the missing amounts in the accounting books. But something seemed off by the look of the invoices, but Inga couldn't place her finger on it. After looking over the details on the invoices, she noticed a pattern. All the missing invoices were linked to funds being sent to the Cayman Islands. That was odd, she thought. She wondered if something strange was going on since the Cayman Islands infamously had offshore accounts and illegal funds. Inga thought she might take these accounting books with her and see if anything seemed odd. So, after making a quick note stating she noticed a discrepancy in one invoice, Inga grabbed the books and made her way to her car, her mind buzzing with questions and suspicions.

38

Ten Years Ago
Friday, August 15, 2014, Evening

When her phone rang, Clara Mateo was lying on her girlfriend's bed, eating popcorn and watching *Mean Girls*. Her girlfriend paused the movie as Clara pulled out her phone to check who was calling. The caller ID read, Aunt Mary. That was odd.

"I think I need to take this. My Aunt Mary is calling. It might be an emergency," she said.

"That's understandable," replied Clara's girlfriend before continuing, "I'm going to go get a refill so you can have some privacy. Do you want anything?"

Clara replied, "No thanks." Her girlfriend nodded in acknowledgment before exiting the room. A moment later, Clara called her aunt back and said, "Good evening, Aunt Mary. Is everything okay?"

Aunt Mary spoke in sobs as she said, "It's your parents. They were in a car accident. The hospital isn't sure they are going to make it. You need to come as soon as possible. Do you have anyone who can give you a ride, or do you need us to call someone to pick you up?"

Clara was on the verge of tears as she said, "My friend can take me. What's the address of the hospital?" After her aunt told her the address, Clara hung up the phone.

A few moments later, her girlfriend returned and said angrily, "I heard you call me your friend to your aunt. Is that what I am to you?"

Clara was torn between her love for Selina and her worry for her parents when she said, "That's not the most important thing at the moment, Selina. Both of my parents are in the hospital and might not make it. We can discuss this later. Right now, I need your support."

Selina looked frustrated as she said, "I know you're right. I just don't want us to have to hide who we are anymore."

Clara felt nervous as she said, "Speaking of not wanting to hide who we are anymore, there is something I want to tell you. But it's going to have to wait for the drive over. We need to get going."

Selina said, "Okay, that's fine. But it's nothing bad, is it?"

"It's nothing bad. Just trust me, okay?"

Selina sighed as she said, "Okay, I trust you. Just give me a couple of minutes to put on my shoes, and I'll be ready to go."

"Thank you," replied the nervous Clara as she waited for her girlfriend to get ready.

A few moments later, they left the house, got into Selina's car, and headed to the hospital. On their way there, Selina asked, "So, what did you want to talk about?"

Clara gulped as she began telling Selina what she needed to tell her, as they made their way to the hospital, hoping her parents would be okay.

39

Present Day
Saturday, August 10, 2024, 2:30 p.m.

Iris watched as the couple stared in shock at her revelation. After a moment, the man said, "That's horrible to have found. Even though the man deserved a worse fate."

Iris stared in surprise as the woman jumped in and said, "I agree. Drowning alone does not suffice for all the harm he has caused in the world."

Iris had to agree, but their reactions seemed too emotional to be unrelated to Charles Underwood. So, she said, "Sorry to pry, but did you two happen to know Charles Underwood personally? Your reactions suggest a deeper connection."

Both people quickly said, "No." However, Iris doubted its sincerity since shortly afterward, the man said, "I'm sorry, Miss, but we must get going. It was nice talking to you." Before the couple ran off.

Iris found it strange that potentially three people had lied about knowing Charles Underwood less than twenty-four hours after his death. There seemed to be more to this story than meets the eye, and she was resolute in her determination to uncover the truth. She also wanted to honor her husband's wishes and close his cold case involving Charles Underwood, a task he had longed to complete. The thought filled her with a mix of determination and sadness. Iris was going to make her husband proud. But first, she needed to devise a game plan. Unfortunately, her three new suspects hadn't revealed their names to her. So that was a dead end. After a few more minutes of contemplation, Iris realized there wasn't much she could do at the moment but relax. So, with that in mind, she thought a little cozy reading in her cabin sounded nice, so she headed back there.

40

Present Day
Saturday, August 10, 2024, 2:45 p.m.

As Iris entered her cabin, she heard the gentle hum of the air conditioning and the distant sound of waves crashing against the ship. She pulled her phone out of her purse, the familiar scent of leather wafting up to her nose, and noticed that her daughter Stella was calling. After answering the call, Iris said, "Good afternoon, Stel. How are you today?"

"I'm doing well. I'm just heading to pick up the kids from school. How is the cruise going so far, Mom?"

Iris considered telling her about Charles Underwood but decided against it, not wanting to burden her daughter. Instead, she said, "Oh, I'm doing all right. I just returned from the gym on the cruise ship."

"Oh, that's awesome. What is your favorite part of the cruise so far?"

"That's tough. The whole thing is very fancy. It's got a salon, a spa, a pool, and lots of good food. It is difficult to choose just one thing."

"I'm glad you're enjoying yourself so far, Mom. Aren't you supposed to land in Barbados tomorrow?"

"I'm not sure. Let me get the brochure real quick," Iris said, getting up and retrieving the brochure before continuing, "I'm back. Let me find the right page…"

After a moment, Iris says, "Aw, here it is. Yes, I will arrive there tomorrow morning unless…"

"Unless what, mom?"

Iris felt a wave of relief as she said, "Oh, nothing, dear. I have to let you go. I think I hear someone knocking on my door."

Stella said a sudden "Goodbye" before Iris hung up.

That was a close one, Iris thought. She'll have to be more careful in the future. Although she was surprised, her son hadn't informed his sister about what she had gotten into yet. Maybe she should talk with him later about not saying anything to Stella about it. She had a lot to deal with, raising those two little children all on her own without worrying about Charles Underwood and the potential trouble her mom might get into. Iris laughed at her own shenanigans. In all the excitement, she had forgotten that she wanted to read and relax before dinner. A nice warm shower, a glass of wine, and a good book afterward sounded good to her, so with that in mind, she headed to the bathroom.

41

Present Day
Saturday, August 10, 2024, 5:15 p.m.

Iris had just gotten out of the shower when she heard a knock on her door. She wondered who it was as she said, "I'll be there in a minute." The knocking stopped. After quickly changing into her clothes, Iris went and answered the door. When she opened the door, the captain surprised her by being there and said, "Sorry to bother you, Miss, but I need to ask you some questions regarding the incident this morning. If it's all right, may I come inside?"

Iris replied, "Sure thing, captain," stepping aside, letting the captain enter, and closing the door. Afterward, she led him to the kitchen bar and asked, "Captain, would you like something to drink?"

"No thanks. If you may, let's get down to business. I wanted to ask if you take *Xanax* or if you have any in your possession."

Iris's face showed confusion as she said, "No, I don't. Why are you asking?"

The captain seemed to hesitate before he said, "Well, our research center found traces of *Xanax* in that bottle of scotch you found at the bottom of the pool. So now we're wondering if someone drugged Charles or if he mixed the two himself. Since you found the body and the bottle, I had to ask you because it's a matter of procedure."

"I understand, captain. But I can assure you I had nothing to do with the *Xanax* or Charles's death. Although I suspected that something shady had occurred since Charles had a sketchy past that had harmed many people, Plus, some people on the ship seemed to act oddly when I mentioned his name today."

The captain raised his voice in dismay as he said, "You talked to people about finding him dead? Are you trying to cause a panic?"

Iris blushed as she said, "No, of course not. I just said they had acted odd at the mention of Charles being aboard the ship. However, he had yelled at a woman named Nora Brooks at dinner last night. I think he might have recognized her as a reporter who had written negative remarks about him shortly after his wife had disappeared about ten years ago. I would ask her and see if you can learn anything from her."

The captain's eyebrows rose in interest as he said, "That is very useful to know. I will definitely ask her those questions. If you learn anything else of importance, please let me know." Then, he retrieved a business card from his pocket, handed it to Iris, and told her, "If you need to reach me, call this number. Until then, I'll bid you adieu." Then he left.

Iris looked at the business card and thought about what had just happened. It seemed like her intuition was right. Someone might have actually killed Charles. But the thought was a little scary. If there was a killer on the cruise, what wouldn't stop them from killing again? She had to be careful. Iris hoped she knew what she was getting into. Maybe she should call her son and update him on the recent developments. It seemed like a good idea, so that's what she did. Unfortunately, the call went to voicemail. So, instead, she left a voicemail and got ready for dinner.

42

Present Day
Saturday, August 10, 2024, 6:15 p.m.

As Iris entered the Mexican restaurant on deck eight, the aroma of sizzling beef mixed with the smell of freshly made tortillas with a hint of salty margaritas made her mouth water as she waited to be seated. A short while later, the hostess led her to a table and handed her a menu. As Iris looked at her menu, her phone rang. She pulled it out of her purse and saw that it was her son. Iris answered it quickly and said, "Good evening, Sammy. I can't talk for long. I'm about to order dinner. How are you?"

"Good evening, mom. I just listened to your voicemail. What recent developments have happened?"

"Well, the captain came by my room earlier and told me they found traces of *Xanax* in the scotch bottle they found at the bottom of the pool, and they suspect potential foul play. Additionally, when I mentioned the name Charles Underwood, some people I encountered today showed strange behavior. There is something suspicious going on."

"Seems like it. However, if Charles was indeed murdered,

as we suspect, you must be cautious and make an effort to stay out of trouble to avoid getting hurt."

Iris sighed relief at the sight of the server returning and said, "Sorry, the server just returned. I've got to go, bye!" before rapidly hanging up.

As Iris finished the last bit of her beef tacos, she took a sip of her strawberry margarita in delight. The food was delicious and authentic. She can't thank her children enough for gifting her this cruise. She would have to get them some nice souvenirs tomorrow in Barbados. But the inner com interrupted her, "Good evening, everyone. This is your captain speaking. I just wanted to make two announcements. The first is that in half an hour, our first round of trivia night starts on deck nine in the lounge area. The second is that we land in Barbados tomorrow at 10 a.m., so make sure you go to bed early so you can be ready for our landing. Tomorrow at 5 p.m., the ship will depart from Barbados, and it won't pick up or refund anyone who missed it, so please ensure you return on time tomorrow. Otherwise, I hope everyone has a good day on the SS Paradise."

Iris had forgotten about trivia night in all the chaos involving Charles Underwood. She wanted to go to that, so she got up and headed back to her room.

43

Present Day
Saturday, August 10, 2024, 7:20 p.m.

Iris entered deck nine and made her way to the lounge area. Once there, she spotted a line of people. She guessed it was for trivia night and got in line. A few moments later, she heard a man's voice at the front of the line ask for someone's name and how many people were on their team, confirming her thoughts. However, it worried Iris since she didn't have anyone to team up with. She hoped that wouldn't be a problem as she waited in line.

Once her turn came, the cruise worker holding the clipboard asked, "What name can I register you as?"

"My name is Iris May."

As the worker's pen glided across the clipboard, he complimented, "That's a lovely name, madam. How many people are in your team, and what is your team's name?"

"Just one person and you can use my first name."

After making some more notes on his clipboard, he said, "All right, I have everything settled. Take a seat, and we will start in a few minutes."

Iris said, "Sounds good," before exiting the line and looking for a place to sit. As she waited, she scanned the group of people that were scattered around to see if she spotted anyone she recognized. After a few moments, she noticed Nora sitting beside the man she had talked to earlier that day at the bar. Iris wondered if they knew each other and if they had any connection to Charles. She also spotted Tyler and Georgia sitting beside each other, talking in another part of the crowd. But just then, she also spotted that young couple from the gym. This should be interesting, she thought as she waited for trivia night to start.

A few minutes later, the worker with the clipboard cleared his throat and said, "Good evening, everyone. I hope you're all doing well. I will be your host tonight for our trivia night. Tonight's categories are on Barbados trivia. The categories can include anything related to music, history, local cuisine, religion, art, festivals, etc. The rules are simple. I will read out a question for you to answer. Once I finish reading it, the first person I see raising their hand will get a chance to answer. If they answer correctly, their team will earn a point. If they answer wrong, then someone else can steal. This will go on for several rounds, and whoever has the most points at the end wins a gift card to use in Barbados tomorrow. Does anyone have questions?" The room was filled with the buzz of anticipation as the participants prepared for the challenge.

After a moment of silence, the announcer continued, "Okay, let us begin…"

Iris wanted to keep a close eye on the people she had recognized as the questions were being asked. But it was hard with all the people gathered at the event. She heard the worker say, "What religion makes up 80% of Barbados?"

Iris goes to raise her hand, but so does Selina at the same time. The announcer says, "Team Selina, what is your answer?"

Selina smiles confidently and replies, "Christianity."

"That's correct. Team Selina gets the point. The next

question is, which singer had their first album, *Music of the Sun*, come out in 2005 and was born in Barbados?"

Iris knew little about pop culture, so she kept her hand down. But she saw Tyler, Georgia, and Nora raise their hands among the crowd. The announcer said, "Team Fashion, what is your answer?"

Tyler replied, "The answer is clearly the goddess Rihanna."

The announcer replied, "That's correct. Round two goes to Team Fashion. The next question is this: what is the name of the Barbadian literary magazine that debuted in the 1940s and 1950s, including the famous writer Derek Wolcott?"

Another pop culture question. Iris didn't know this answer either, so she kept her hand down again. Nora was the only person she recognized who raised their hand out of a group of strangers. The announcer called on Nora, and she said, "The answer is Bim."

The announcer replied, "That's correct. Team News gets one point. Our next question is this: What popular attraction commonly found in Las Vegas is prohibited in Barbados?"

Georgia raised her hand to answer and got called on. She says, "Is the answer strip clubs?"

The announcer replies, "Sorry, that is incorrect." Then he called on Jordan and said, "Team Selina, what is your answer?"

Jordan smiles confidently before saying, "The correct answer is casinos."

The announcer shouts, "That's correct. Two points for Team Selina. Here's our next question: What is Barbados known as the capital of?"

Iris thought she might know this answer, so she raised her hand. Sandy and Selina also raised their hands. The announcer called on Sandy. He replied, "I think the answer is ginger halibut?"

The announcer said dramatically, "Unfortunately, that is incorrect. Team Selina, what is the answer?"

Jordan smiled, saying, "The answer is Cou-Cou with flying fish."

The announcer replies, "That's correct, putting Team Selina in the lead with three points. This is our last question. Name a popular game played in Barbados that uses the phrase, slamming a dom?"

Georgia, Selina, Nora, and Iris, among a few other strangers, raised their hands. The announcer calls on Iris.

Iris replied, "I believe the answer is dominos."

The announcer states, "That's correct—one point for Team Iris. That wraps up our trivia night. And our winner is Team Selina with three points!" The entire group clapped as the announcer continued, "Please come up and claim your $100 Visa gift card. Regarding the rest of our contestants, drinks are being served at the bar for those who want to stay."

As the trivia night concluded, Iris made her way to the winners, a sense of familiarity tugging at her. The woman's name, Selina, sparked a memory but remained just out of reach. She hoped learning her partner's name might provide a clue. The anticipation of uncovering the connection, coupled with the winners' reaction to her, kept her curiosity piqued.

Once she got to them, Iris noticed a momentary shock on both of their faces before quickly returning to a smile. How interesting, she thought as she approached them and said, "Congratulations on winning the trivia night, guys."

Selina replied curtly, "Oh, thanks, Miss."

Iris caught the sarcasm as she said, "I believe we chatted earlier, but I didn't catch your names."

Selina spoke in a clipped tone, saying, "My name is Selina, and this is my fiancé, Jordan."

"Nice to meet you guys. I won't keep you. I just wanted to congratulate you on your win."

However, before she could walk away, Jordan asked, "Before you leave, I was just wondering what your name is?"

Iris smiled and said, "My name is Iris May," before turning to leave.

44

Present Day
Saturday, August 10, 2024, 8:45 p.m.

As Iris approached her cabin, eagerness flowed through her. She couldn't wait to look over her late husband's old case files as she unlocked the door and entered her cabin. Once inside, Iris went to her coffee machine, poured out the morning's brew, and started a fresh pot. Afterward, she sat down at the bar and opened her email. A smile came to her face when she saw her son's email. When Iris clicked on it, she crossed her fingers as she watched it slowly download onto her screen. While she waited, Iris went and checked on her coffee. It was done, so she poured herself a cup before returning to check on the progress.

Upon her return, she was pleasantly surprised to discover that the file had been successfully downloaded. After setting her coffee cup on the bar, Iris looked through some of the case files. Since the cases were written chronologically, Iris found that most of the initial information was old news. But as Iris scrolled down the pages, she saw some new information.

She noticed three new points of interest. The first point of interest was that Stacy had a younger sister named Mary, who became a recluse after Stacy disappeared. Iris wondered where Mary was now and made a mental note to look into that later.

The second point of interest was that Charles had been seen leaving a strip club called *Long Legs* shortly after his wife had disappeared. Iris wondered if he had been having an affair with one of the exotic dancers at the club before his wife had disappeared. She would have to check and see if the club was still around, and if so, maybe she could get her son to see if anyone remembered anything that happened back then.

The last thing to note is that Inga named her daughter Selina. Iris wondered if that girl who won the trivia night with her boyfriend could be the daughter of Charles Underwood's murdered administrative assistant. The odds were slim, but if she was, that added a second person connected to Charles Underwood aboard the ship. The more Iris looked into things, the more she became convinced that someone had murdered Charles. But the question was, how did that person lead Charles to the pool deck and get him to drink that scotch bottle laced with *Xanax*? That was still a piece of the puzzle she hadn't figured out yet. Maybe she would learn something tomorrow to help get her closer to solving that problem. But for now, she needed to wind down for the night. So, she closed the email and headed to her bedroom.

Once there, she turned on the TV, put on the movie *Clue*, and lay back in bed. As she watched the movie, her eyes grew heavy. Before she knew it, she fell fast asleep.

45

Ten Years Ago
Thursday, August 28, 2014, Evening

Iris was peeling potatoes over her pull-out trash can in the kitchen as she listened to *Don't Stop Believing* on the radio. After she finished, she put the potatoes in the fry cutter. As she diced them up, Iris listened to *Living on A Prayer*, silently humming along to the beat.

After she finished, Iris dumped the fries into a pot of grease that she turned on medium before getting the hamburger out of the refrigerator. She removed the pre-made patties from the container and placed a few on the pan as she turned up the heat.

A short while later, the food was ready. Iris placed the fries on a plate to cool in the microwave before covering the hamburgers. Once she finished, she turned off the radio and switched on her kitchen TV. Nancy Grace popped on screen with the headline, *Real Estate Tycoon Charles Underwood seen leaving strip club shortly after wife disappears*.

Iris thought that looked bad for him as she watched the program. Nancy said that an anonymous tip sent in this video footage of Charles leaving the strip club, *Long Legs*, only weeks after his wife had mysteriously disappeared. Rumors stated Charles had been going there before his wife had disappeared. Nancy speculated that perhaps Charles had gotten infatuated with one dancer there, and his wife had found out. It wouldn't be the first time, Iris thought. She was glad her husband hadn't done anything foolish like that.

A few minutes later, Iris heard the door open. She turned off the TV as she heard her husband say, "Good evening, babe. How are you doing?"

Iris smiled and turned to face her husband, saying, "I'm doing well. I listened to Nancy Grace while waiting for you to get home. Have you recently heard about Charles being spotted outside a strip club?"

"Yes, we just found out earlier today. I knew that creep was up to no good. It wouldn't surprise me if he got rid of his wife so he could be with some young dancer at the club. However, we have no proof so far."

"Well, regardless, it doesn't make his character look good. Dinner is ready whenever. However, I might need to warm up the fries in the air fryer. Let me check."

"I guess you made hamburgers for dinner then."

Iris shouted, "Yes, that's right," from the kitchen as she opened the microwave to check the fries. After checking their warmth, she continued, "They could use a few minutes in the air fryer. You could go shower."

Henry entered the kitchen and said, "Sounds like a good idea. I'll return in a few minutes to join you for dinner."

"Sounds good, dear," Iris said before Henry took off to shower.

46

Present Day
Sunday, August 11, 2024, 8:15 a.m.

Iris slowly opened her eyes to the familiar sound of her alarm going off. After reaching to turn it off, she stretched and rose from the bed. Grabbing some clean clothes from her travel bag, Iris went to shower.

After her invigorating shower, Iris entered the kitchen and started a pot of coffee, the aroma filling the air. While waiting for it to brew, Iris flipped through the ship's itinerary. Locating the stewardess's call number, she dialed and waited for the line to answer, the ship's gentle hum providing a soothing background.

A moment later, Iris heard a woman on the other line say, "Good morning. My name is Joanne. How may I serve you?"

"Good morning, Joanne. If it's all right, I'd like to order room service."

"Of course, Miss. Do you know what you want?"

"Actually, can you tell me what is available?"

"Sure thing, Hun. Here is a list of common breakfast orders we receive…"

The number of options surprised Iris. After a moment of consideration, she said, "I think I'll have some scrambled eggs, a few slices of bacon, and some toast with jam, please."

"Certainly, Miss. Your order will be ready in about thirty minutes. Is that acceptable?"

"Sounds perfect. Thanks for your help."

Joanne replied cheerfully, "No problem, Miss. I'll bring your food up shortly," she said before hanging up the phone.

With that out of the way, Iris checked on her coffee. It was done, so she poured herself a cup before returning to the bar. As she sipped on her coffee, she flipped through the itinerary again, her heart fluttering with excitement. This time, she wanted to see what it had to say about Barbados. A few pages in, she found a little guide detailing potential sights to check out. As she scanned through the listed options, she saw that there was a very popular shopping district called Bridgetown. She thought that would be a good place to shop for souvenirs, a thought that brought a smile to her face. They also listed a well-known beach called Carlisle Bay. It looked nice from the pictures, but Iris doubted she would go there. The brochure also talked about their famous rum bars. She thought that might be a good place to get some native rum for her son since he was a spirit collector. The only other place of interest was a church called St. John's Parish. That caught her eye. It held some interesting history, apparently. Plus, she felt it was something she and her husband would have checked out if he were still alive. She would definitely have to check that out if she got the chance. A knock on the door interrupted her thoughts. So, Iris got up and answered the door, her mind still buzzing with the possibilities of the day ahead.

Opening the door, she saw a woman dressed in a red uniform with gold trim. Iris assumed this was Joanne. A silver name tag confirmed her thoughts. She stood outside with a cart that housed a giant silver platter. Joanne smiled as she said, "Room service for Iris May," her voice warm and friendly.

"That's me," replied Iris with a friendly smile, her voice filled with warmth and gratitude.

"Good," Joanne said, removing a bill from her pocket with a pen. She said, "Please sign here, Miss, so that we can charge this to your room."

Iris did as she was told. Then the woman said, "Okay, here you go," as she handed Iris the platter before continuing, "I'll come and pick up the dirty stuff later today. Just leave it in the sink."

"Sounds good," replied Iris as Joanne turned around and left with her cart. Then she returned inside with her food.

Back at the bar, she ate her breakfast in silence, enjoying every bite. She wondered how much this meal had cost her, but the taste was worth every penny. After she had finished, she placed the platter in the sink and checked the clock. It was 9:30 a.m. It was almost time for the ship to dock in Barbados. So, Iris grabbed her purse before making her way to the bridge, the anticipation of the day's adventures making her steps lighter.

On the bridge, Iris spotted Nora conversing with the man she had been partnered with on trivia night. Iris couldn't help but wonder about his name, so she discreetly made her way closer, her curiosity piqued.

Once there, Iris overheard Nora saying, "So, Sandy, how does Carlisle Bay sound to you?"

So, his name is Sandy, she thought, a small victory in her quest to know more about her fellow passengers. That was a start, but she wasn't sure what good it would do her without knowing his last name as she listened to more of their conversation. She heard Sandy say, "Sounds good to me, Nora. I haven't been scuba diving in a long time. You might have to show me the ropes again."

But then the two stepped away, and Iris couldn't hear anymore. But it was interesting to learn that Nora and Sandy knew how to scuba dive. That could be fun to try, Iris mused, her mind already imagining the underwater world of Carlisle Bay. If she had time today, she could check out Carlisle Bay and see what Nora and Sandy were up to, a thought that filled her with a sense of adventure.

A few moments later, the captain arrived and announced that the ship would soon pull into port. Iris scanned the other passengers while she waited in anticipation. She spotted Selina and Jordan talking in the corner. She wondered where they were going today. As the ship pulled into port, Iris couldn't help but wonder where Georgia and Tyler were headed since she hadn't seen them anywhere.

47

Present Day
Sunday, August 11, 2024, 10:00 a.m.

Iris followed the other passengers as they walked down the gangplank and onto the pier in Barbados. Once on the pier, she took in the salty sea air as she noticed that the port was full of various ships of different shapes and sizes, each docked in various slips. But from the look of things, the SS Paradise was one of the bigger ships docked there. Once again, as she walked down the pier, she wondered how much this trip had cost her kids.

At the end of the dock, she spotted some benches. Iris walked over and sat down at an empty one before pulling out her phone to look up the phone number for a taxi. After a few minutes of searching, she found one for a service in the area. After making the call, she waited for the taxi to arrive.

After getting in the taxi, the driver asked, "Where are you headed, Miss?"

"St. John's Parish, please."

"Sure thing. If you're interested, I can be your tour guide, for just $10 more."

Iris, her curiosity piqued, pondered for a moment before responding, "Sure. Could you enlighten me with some intriguing history and captivating highlights of Barbados?"

"Of course, Miss. I'll start off with St. John's Parish since that's where we're headed. It's an old Gothic building built on the East Coast. It also houses the gravesite of a descendant of Emperor Constantine and has one of the only two sundials on the island."

"That's very interesting. What information can you provide about Carlisle Bay?"

"That's a very popular tourist sight. It's also a protected marine area that has a scuba diving site. It's a good place to see some shipwrecks and things of that nature. It is also close to Bridgetown, which is the capital of Barbados."

"Carlisle Bay sounds beautiful and mysterious. I might have to check it out. But you mentioned Bridgetown. I was considering going there. Can you tell me more about what they have there?"

"Sure thing. It's a hot spot for restaurants and shops. It also houses some of our famous rum shops."

"I read about those. I considered going there to get some rum for my son back home. Do you have any suggestions on which one I should go to?"

"I would suggest *Malcolm's Rum Pub*. It looks worn down, but the rum and service are great."

"I'll have to keep that in mind. Thank you for the recommendation!"

"No problem, Miss. It seems we have arrived at the church."

Iris looked out the window in surprise. That was a quick ride, she thought as she watched the taxi park outside St. John's Parish.

48

Present Day
Sunday, August 11, 2024, 10:20 a.m.

Paying the taxi driver, Iris exited and gazed at the gothic masterpiece before her as she approached the building. St. John's Parish had solid gray stone walls that spiraled high into the sky, and guarding the left side of the entrance of the front door was a breathtaking religious sculpture. Iris thought the sight was beautiful and knew her husband would have enjoyed it too as she entered the church.

As she entered, Iris spotted a small side table covered in pamphlets. That could be useful, she mused as she walked over and retrieved one. After flipping through it, a few things caught her eye. British sculptor Richard Westmacott made the statue out front. She also saw an excerpt about the gravesite of Ferdinando Palaeologus, who was the descendant of Emperor Constantine, as the taxi driver mentioned. She also saw an image of the sundial the taxi driver talked about.

After putting the pamphlet in her purse, Iris walked around the church, taking in the sights. But as she entered the graveyard, a shock ran through her when she saw Selina and

Jordan talking by Ferdinando Palaeologus's gravesite. She wanted to see what they were discussing, so she slowly approached the couple. But as she got closer, Selina turned around and faced Iris. With shock on her face, she said, "Oh, hi there, Iris. Fancy meeting you here!"

Jordan turned to face Iris as she said, "Hello, you guys. Funny coincidence. What brings you to St. John's Parish?"

Selina spoke excitedly as she raised her hand, revealing a shiny diamond engagement ring. "Well, my fiancé and I were checking this church out to see if we might have our wedding here. Since Jordan has family here in Barbados."

Iris smiled as she said, "How exciting. How long have the two of you been together?"

Selina replied, "Almost ten years."

How interesting, Iris thought. Iris went out on a limb and said, "That's a really long time together. Congrats on your engagement. Not to get off-topic, but are you related to Inga Lagman?"

Selina's face turned pale as she asked, "Why do you ask that?"

"Well, you have the same name as her daughter, and you seem to hold a grudge against Charles Underwood, so it would make sense if you were Inga's daughter."

Jordan's face was red as he said, "Leave my fiancé alone. Why would you bring up something so painful when we're trying to celebrate our engagement on this luxurious trip we won?"

"I'm sorry, I was just wondering because there are suspicions about Charles being murdered. If Selina is Inga's daughter, then she would have a motive for killing him."

The couple's shock was obvious as Selina uttered, "What do you mean Charles is suspected of being murdered?"

"The captain came to me and said Charles had an overdose of *Xanax* mixed with alcohol. He thinks someone might have drugged him."

"That's crazy," Selina shouted before lowering her voice, "It was probably an unfortunate accident."

Jordan said, "That's right, it must have been an accident. Anyway, we have to go now," before he took Selina by the hand and tugged her away.

That certainly stirred them up, mused Iris. She wondered if she had made a mistake by telling them that Charles might have been murdered. Only time would tell, she supposed. But for now, she thought it would be a good time to go somewhere else. As she walked back to the front of the church, Iris called a taxi to come pick her up. As she waited, Iris debated where to go next. Since she still needed to get some souvenirs, Iris guessed she should go to Bridgetown. So, that was her next destination. A few moments later, the taxi pulled up in front of her.

49

Present Day
Sunday, August 11, 2024, 11:15 a.m.

Half an hour later, Iris arrived in Bridgetown. Walking down Broad Street, Iris took in the hordes of shops surrounding her. Walking down the road, she spotted banks, department stores, jewelry shops, and even a mall. After checking out the sights, Iris randomly entered one shop and started exploring. As she walked around, she took in the various wares laid out among the throngs of people walking through the aisles, picking up and examining items before placing them in their shopping carts or returning them to the shelves. After getting her fill, Iris left the store and continued down the street. This pattern continued for a while until she heard her belly rumble with hunger. Time for lunch, she thought. After looking up the nearest restaurants on her phone, Iris settled on one called *Surf and Turf* and made her way there.

The smell of fresh seafood mixed with the scent of beef greeted Iris as she entered the restaurant. The aroma was enticing and held up to the restaurant's name, *Surf and Turf*. As she walked up to the host's stand, the host quickly seated Iris in a booth and handed her a menu. After glancing at the menu, Iris decided on a sweet tea and a seafood platter comprising shrimp, scallops, and lobster with a side salad. A few moments later, the server came by and took her order. After he left, Iris went to wash her hands.

On her way back from the bathroom, Iris spotted Nora eating lunch with Sandy in a corner booth. Based on the animated gestures Iris saw, the two seemed to enjoy each other's company. What were the odds of running into them here? She wondered as she returned to her booth.

As she sat back down, Iris thought now would be a good time to do a little research since she had stable Wi-Fi and was waiting for her lunch to arrive. Since she just confirmed that Selina was Inga's daughter, Iris researched her and Jordan. After opening *Google* and doing a quick search through *Facebook*, she learned Selina has family in Switzerland and that her fiancé Jordan's last name was Mateo. Switching gears, Iris clicked on Jordan's profile. After a quick scroll, she saw Jordan did indeed have family living in Barbados. But before she could continue, the server returned with her food, and Iris switched her focus on her lunch.

The food was delicious and fresh, and Iris sat with a full stomach and a smile on her face. As she paid the bill, she tried to take a sneak peek to see if Nora and Sandy were still at the restaurant but couldn't find them. She guessed they must have paid and left already. Iris wondered if she would run into them again as she returned outside.

With a sense of adventure, Iris followed the taxi driver's suggestion and visit the rum shop. She pulled out her phone and quickly located it on *Google Maps*. The ten-minute walk seemed like a small price to pay for the promise of a new experience. Iris set off, her heart filled with anticipation for what the next chapter of her Bridgetown exploration might bring.

50

Present Day
Sunday, August 11, 2024, 1:30 p.m.

Iris stood outside the rum shop. It was easy to spot because of its tall gabled roof and three doors at the front that made up its entrance. Iris liked the homemade sign-out front that read *Malcolm's Rum Pub* in faded colors, plus the assortment of bright colors that make up the building itself. She felt that the overall result was an old and familiar feeling, like a cozy place to go hang out with no worries. The sight pulled Iris in like a moth to a flame as she entered the building.

Stepping into the pub, Iris was greeted by a warm and friendly atmosphere. The simple design, with a counter for serving guests and a few wooden barstools lined up outside it, was complemented by the energetic and upbeat patrons. They chatted over tiny sandwiches and other small snacks, creating a friendly buzz. Iris felt a sense of belonging as she made her way to the bar.

As she approached the bar, Iris noticed a familiar face sitting on a barstool. She saw Tyler sipping on a cocktail while chatting with a bronze-colored man with short, curly hair. Iris thought now would be a good chance to talk to Tyler. But as she approached Tyler, she overheard him say, "So you like to work out then, Philip? I like that in a man."

Then Iris heard Philip reply, "Yeah, I do. Perhaps I could show off my muscles sometime then."

But before he could continue, Iris, her foot catching on a loose floorboard, stumbled forward and collided with Tyler, causing him to lurch out of his chair and almost topple to the ground. Mortified by her clumsiness, Iris stammered, "I'm so sorry, Tyler. Are you all right?" as she reached out to help him.

After taking her hand and standing back up, he said, "Yeah, I'm okay. Thanks for asking."

Then Philip said, "Glad you're okay, Tyler," before he flashed a smile.

Iris felt like she was interrupting something, so she said, "If I'm..."

But before she got to finish, the bartender came over and said, "Philip, your break is over, so please stop flirting with the guests and get back to work."

This caused Philip to blush before saying, "Sorry, Tyler, I have duties to attend to," before getting up and heading around the bar.

Tyler's face fell momentarily, his eyes betraying a hint of disappointment as he took a sip from his drink. Iris, feeling a pang of guilt, said, "I'm sorry for interrupting your date, Tyler."

Tyler threw his head back in laughter before saying, "No problem, girlfriend. You know how it is. Men come and go like a warm summer breeze. Besides, it's not the first time that has happened on this trip. Anyway, how are you doing?"

Iris didn't share Tyler's view of people coming and going, but she knew it was tough for gay men to find a partner based on her son's past dating experiences. Maybe she should tell Tyler about her son. However, Iris realized her son had warned her about trying to play matchmaker in his dating life. But she felt Tyler might be her son's type since Tyler was a thin, light blonde, wore diamond earrings, and had a big personality. Well, it wouldn't hurt to mention, she thought, plus now would be an excellent way to get Tyler to open up before she tried asking more about Georgia's connection to Charles Underwood. So, she said, "I'm doing all right. I've just been trying to find a good souvenir for my children back home. Maybe you could help me, Tyler."

This caused Tyler to raise his eyebrows before saying, "Well, if you got a cute gay son who needs a boyfriend, I could be his souvenir."

Iris laughed as she said, "Actually, my son is gay and single, but I was thinking more like alcohol suggestions."

Tyler laughed and replied, "I can help with that too. If it's rum you're looking for, I would have to suggest *Mount Gay Rum*."

"Hilarious, Tyler. That's a good one. But seriously, do you know any real rum brands I can get for my son?"

Tyler dramatically held his hand to his face as if offended by this comment before saying, "That's rude of you to say. If you don't believe me, ask the bartender to see if it's real."

Iris played along and said, "Sure thing, I'll ask the bartender then," before she waved over the bartender.

Once he arrived, he said, "What can I get you, Madame?"

Iris replied, "I wanted to know if you had any *Mount Gay Rum*?"

"Yes, we do. What size bottle do you want? We have a mini, a flask, and a pint and a half."

Iris thought about it momentarily, trying to decide what she should get. But ultimately, she got the biggest bottle since her son was kind enough to help pay for her trip. So, she said, "I'll take the pint and a half, please." The bartender nodded his head before going to retrieve the bottle.

Once he returned, he placed the bottle on the counter and said, "Here you go. That will be $20. Also, I'll need to see your driver's license." So, Iris pulled her wallet out of her purse to retrieve her credit card and driver's license. After locating both, she handed them over to the bartender. After glancing over her license, he returned it to her and said, "Thanks, Madame. I'll go get your receipt." Then he took off with her credit card.

A few moments later, he returned carrying a receipt and pen and said, "Please sign this, Madame," before handing them over. Iris signed and added a small tip before returning the copy to him. This led him to say, "Thanks for the business, Madame. Would you like a bag for your bottle?"

Iris smiled, "Yes, please. I would appreciate it." So, he went and fetched her a bag. When he returned, he placed the bottle inside and handed it to her.

After Iris took it, the bartender said, "Is there anything else I can get you?"

Iris replied, "No thanks, I'm good." The bartender nodded before taking off, leaving Iris alone with Tyler.

"See, I told you it was real," began Tyler.

Iris laughed while saying, "Okay, you were right. I'm sorry for not believing you. What can I do to make it up to you?"

Tyler gave a sly grin before saying, "Well, if you want, you could show me a picture of your son. I'm curious to see what he looks like."

Iris played along as she said, "Sure thing, I always like to show off my babies." She retrieved her phone and opened her photo gallery and pulled up a picture of her son on the 4th of July, saying, "Here you go," and handed it over to him.

Tyler studied the image before saying, "Dang, he looks fine. Would it be all right if I gave you my number to give him?"

Iris grinned, saying, "Sure, I don't mind, but I can't promise he'll reach out. That's up to him."

Tyler enthusiastically said, "That's understandable. I'll give you one of my business cards so you can tell him to check out my business."

This new information intrigued Iris, so she asked, "What kind of job do you have, Tyler?"

Tyler grinned and said, "I work for a company called *Doll Face*. It's a makeup company similar to *CoverGirl*. I work in a higher-up position, so I handle the advertising part of the company. My best friend Georgia is a model for their sister company, *Southern Belles*. So sometimes we get to work together, which is nice."

Iris thought that working with your best friend sounded nice. But she still had unanswered questions, so she said, "That sounds nice being able to work with your best friend. But I was curious to hear more about what Georgia meant when she said that she and Charles Underwood had a falling out in the past."

"Why are you interested in learning about that? It happened a long time ago."

"Well, the captain came to me and told me he thinks someone might have drugged Charles before he drowned. So, I was wondering if someone had a connection to something in his past."

"That's crazy, girlfriend. That certainly changes things. I'm assuming they don't think it's an accident then."

"The captain seemed to think that was the case, but they will have to investigate further."

"Terrible business, it sounds like. But I can assure you, Georgia didn't do it. We have been friends for almost ten years, and I can't see her acting like that. Besides, we won this trip in a contest, so I don't see how she could have planned something like that, anyway."

How intriguing, Iris pondered. This was the second time she had heard about a group of people winning a trip on this cruise. What were the odds, she wondered. But before she could delve deeper into her thoughts, Tyler's phone interrupted. "Excuse me," he said, answering the call. A few moments later, he said, "Sorry about that. Georgia needs my help with a fashion emergency, so I have to go."

"I understand. It was nice talking to you, Tyler. Take care."

Tyler seemed relieved as he said, "Thanks for understanding, girlfriend." Then, he got up from his seat. But then stopped midway and said, "I almost forgot to give you my business card." So, he went and retrieved one from his wallet and said, "Here you go. Also, do you have a pen?"

Iris laughed, "Of course, I have a pen. I am a mom, after all." Tyler laughed as Iris pulled a pen out of her purse and handed it to him. Then, he wrote his name and number on the back of the business card. Despite being a man, Iris found herself surprised by the neatness of Tyler's signature.

After a moment, he finished. He returned the pen, handed her his card, and winked. "Thanks for the pen. Make sure you give that to your son."

Iris replied, "No problem, and I will. Take care, Tyler." He smiled and said, "I plan to," before getting up and leaving.

51

Present Day
Sunday, August 11, 2024, 2:30 p.m.

Iris sat at the bar in the rum shop, trying to figure out her next move. She still needed to get something for her daughter, but she wasn't sure where to go or what to get. Since she was in a foreign country, Iris decided the best course of action was to ask the bartender for suggestions. So, she waved him over and said, "Excuse me, sir, but I was wondering if you could help me. I want to get my daughter a souvenir, but I'm unsure where to go."

The bartender enthusiastically replied, "Sure thing. What kind of things does your daughter like?"

Iris thought briefly before saying, "Well, Stella enjoys cooking and spicy foods and spices. Do you know where I could get some local spices to take home with me?"

The bartender laughed as he said, "Well, that's an easy problem to solve. If you want to get some spicy local spices, I suggest you go to *James's supermarket* in Bridgetown and pick up some *Delish Bajan* seasoning, which comes in jars. Or you can pick up some *Aunt May's Bajan* pepper sauce. Both are hot and good on a variety of things."

Iris chuckled, a spark of excitement in her eyes. "How amusing that *Bajan* pepper sauce shares my last name, May. It's a sign, I suppose. I'll definitely have to pick some up. Thank you for the tip."

"No problem. If it has your name in it, it sounds like it was meant to be. Plus, I bet your daughter will get a kick out of it, too."

"I think she will too. Also, before I forget, can you give me directions to the supermarket?"

"Sure thing. Here is how to get there…" After getting the directions, Iris smiled and thanked him before taking off.

Locating the supermarket was more difficult than Iris had been told. Guess a sense of direction doesn't improve with age, she thought as she continued to search for it. By the time Iris had located it, her feet were killing her. Hopefully, she would have better luck finding *Aunt May's Bajan* pepper sauce, but knowing her luck, perhaps not. But the only way to know for sure was to try. So, Iris entered the supermarket to begin her search for her treasure.

Locating the sauce wasn't as tricky as Iris expected. However, the size of the bottle surprised her. It was in a thinner bottle, which made Iris think of those one-liter bottles. Because of this, she imagined you were only supposed to use a small amount at a time. Regardless, Iris hoped her daughter would enjoy it. After grabbing the bottle, she headed towards the checkout aisles. But on her way there, Iris saw Georgia checking out a rack of celebrity gossip magazines. How perfect, Iris thought. This would be an excellent chance to question Georgia more about her connection to Charles. So, she walked over, tapped Georgia on the shoulder, and said, "Hi there, Georgia. What are you looking at?"

Georgia jumped a little in response. After a moment, she

regained her composure and said, "Oh, hi there, Iris. I didn't see you there, sweetheart. I was checking out the local celebrity gossip magazines to see what clothes they wore because it helped me with my job at *Southern Belles*, where I work as a model. But how are you doing?"

Iris found this an excellent time to ask Georgia more about her job at *Southern Belles*. So, she said, "I'm doing all right. I just came to get some of this," holding up the bottle of *Aunt May's Bajan* pepper sauce before continuing, "For my daughter as a souvenir because she likes spicy stuff. But I'm curious to hear more about your job at *Southern Belles*. What exactly do you do there?"

Georgia raised her eyebrows at this question as she said, "I'm surprised you're interested in my job, sugar. I work as a model on one of those runways. But it's not as glamorous as you might think. Not all that glitters is gold, as my Mama used to say."

Iris was very interested to hear this. It seemed like Georgia might dislike her job. But what did that connect to Charles? Iris wasn't sure; maybe her career had nothing to do with it, but Tyler had mentioned Georgia had some past connection. But what type of connection, she wondered. Perhaps she should ask Georgia and see what she says. In the worst-case scenario, Georgia shuts down and walks away. But if Iris gets lucky, she might learn more about Charles and the people he associates with. Plus, she wouldn't know unless she tried, so she took a chance and said, "Speaking of not all that glitters is gold, I was wondering about your past connection to Charles Underwood. From my understanding, you two didn't end things on good terms; why was that?"

Georgia's face turned pale for a second. Then it switched and turned red and flushed.

"How dare you come and ask me personal questions like that? It is none of your business about what our relationship was like or ended. Now, excuse me, I have some things to do."

Iris watched Georgia return the magazine to the shelf

before stomping off like a vindictive woman on the warpath. That touched a nerve, Iris thought. The question was why. Maybe she would learn that answer later that week. But for now, she needed to pay for this sauce before going to her next destination.

52

Present Day
Sunday, August 11, 2024

After paying for her purchases, Iris stood outside the supermarket, wondering where to head next. Maybe she should check Carlisle Bay. Otherwise, she would run out of time before returning to the ship at 5:00 p.m. Since she wasn't ready to return, Iris called a taxi. After finishing her call, she waited by the curb at the supermarket's entrance.

About fifteen minutes later, the taxi pulled into the parking lot and approached Iris. However, right before it reached her, Iris felt a sudden, sharp push from behind, the force propelling her towards the oncoming car. Thankfully, the driver stopped just in time, the screech of the brakes piercing the air. After the shock faded, she thought to turn around and face her attacker. But of course, nobody was there. However, Iris spotted a small object on the ground. She bent to pick it up and noticed it was a business card for Sandy Stone. Upon closer inspection, she also noticed that it said he was a private investigator. How interesting, she thought. That made Iris wonder if someone hired him to keep tabs on

Charles or if Charles himself had hired him to monitor someone else. But regardless, she wondered why he had tried to push her into the street.

A moment later, the taxi driver, a burly man with a thick beard and a friendly smile, got out and said, "Are you all right, Miss? I saw someone push you into the street."

After gathering her bearings, Iris said, "I think I'm all right, but did you see who tried to push me in front of you?"

The taxi driver replied with concern in his voice, "No, Miss, I didn't. They were wearing a big floppy sun hat, sunglasses, and a scarf. But if I had to guess, I would say it was most likely a woman. Should I call the police?"

This statement made Iris need clarification. If Sandy wasn't the one who pushed her, then who did? Her mind raced with possibilities. Plus, why did they have Sandy's business card? It didn't make any sense. But if the driver was right, and it was a woman, it could only have been one of three people: Georgia, Selina, or Nora. But the question was who and why. Iris knew she had ticked off Georgia and Selina both today with her questioning, so both were valid options. On the other hand, Iris hadn't seen much of Nora that day, but she knew Nora acted afraid and avoidant when she brought up the subject of Charles, so she couldn't dismiss Nora either. She planned to question each of them later and see where they claimed to be when she was pushed. She reasoned it probably wouldn't lead anywhere, but it couldn't hurt. But it made her realize that someone had felt threatened enough to get rid of her, which meant that she had to have been right about Charles being murdered. But she still didn't know why. Maybe she should talk to the captain when she returned to the ship and tell him what happened. But just then, her thoughts got interrupted by the taxi driver saying, "Excuse me, Miss. Are you all right? You zoned out for a minute."

Iris blushed and replied, "Sorry, I got distracted, but I don't think you need to call the police. There's nothing they could do, considering neither of us saw who it was." She tried to sound calm and composed, but her voice betrayed a hint of fear.

The taxi driver said, "I guess you make a good point. I'm sorry I couldn't help much."

"No worries, it's not your fault. Although I think I want you to take me to Carlisle Bay if that's all right?"

"Sure thing, Miss. If you're sure, you're okay."

Iris smiled pleasantly before saying, "I'm sure," before getting into the taxi. This led the driver to take her to Carlisle Bay.

A few minutes later, the taxi pulled and parked at Carlisle Bay, and Iris paid her taxi fare. But before she got out of the taxi, she said, "Please wait a moment. I might return and have you take me somewhere else."

The taxi driver replied, "Sure thing, Miss, but I can only wait ten minutes at most."

Iris smiled and said, "That's fine. I plan to be back by then," before getting out of the taxi. Then she went to scan the beach for any sign of Nora or Sandy. However, after searching for a few minutes, Iris realized they were nowhere to be found, so she returned to the taxi. Once inside, she said, "Sorry for the wasted trip. Can you take me to the pier where the cruise ships are docked?"

The driver nodded and started the engine, but Iris couldn't shake the feeling that she was being watched as they drove away.

"Of course, Miss," he said before taking off.

53

Present Day
Sunday, August 11, 2024, 4:00 p.m.

After Iris returned to her cabin and dropped off her things, she pulled out the business card the captain gave her and called him. After a few rings, she heard him say, "Good afternoon, Iris. What can I do for you?"

"Good afternoon, captain. Some important things came up today in Barbados, and I would like to discuss them with you. Can you please come to my room to talk in person?"

"Certainly! Give me a few minutes to finish up some work, and I'll be right over."

Iris replied, "Sounds good. I'll see you then," before hanging up.

About fifteen minutes later, Iris heard a knock on her door. She eagerly answered it. After stepping inside and closing the door, the captain asked, "So what happened?"

"Someone tried to push me in front of my taxi about an hour ago. I think it's because I was talking about the death of Charles."

"That's horrible. I'm glad you're okay. But why were you

talking to people about Charles when I said to keep it on the down low for now?"

"I'm sorry, but other people were asking about what happened at the pool, and I was curious to learn what they had to say. My husband was the lead investigator on the case of Charles's missing wife, Stacy, almost ten years ago, and I know that if he were still here, Henry would have done the same."

The captain sighed as he said, "That complicates things. I can understand you feeling obligated to honor your late husband's memory, but you're not a detective, and you almost got hurt. You need to leave this matter alone. I have an official detective coming on board to investigate the case, so don't worry about it getting solved."

Iris huffed as she said, "Okay, I understand. I'll let the professionals handle it. But when the detective arrives, can you ask them to come and talk to me so I can tell them what I have learned so far? I might have useful information."

"Don't worry, they will talk to you. You are a suspect, after all. You have a connection to Charles, plus you found the body. They will want to hear what you have to say. But don't go nosing around anymore for your own safety."

"I understand, captain."

"Good, I hope so. I got to get going. Take care now."

Iris murmured, "Goodbye," as the captain left her cabin.

54

Present Day
Sunday, August 11, 2024, 4:30 p.m.

Shortly after the captain left, Iris sat at the bar brainstorming her next move as she sipped a glass of red wine from the minibar. She realized she needed to learn more about some of her suspects. So, she pulled out her phone and loaded *Google*. Thankfully, it was working well. Iris assumed this was because the ship was still in port. Whom to search first? She wondered. Since it seemed like a woman had tried to push her into the street, Iris reasoned she should focus on her three female suspects. Georgia came to mind since she hadn't learned much about her yet. So, that was where she started her search.

As Iris scrolled through *Facebook*, she saw many photos of Georgia dressed in various dresses advertising the company she worked for, *Southern Belles*. She also saw many pictures of her with Tyler, which made sense to Iris since they claimed to be best friends. As Iris scrolled back in time, one post caught her eye. It was for a charity event for the *March of Dimes*, which raised money for mothers of babies born either with health problems or passed shortly after their birth. Iris thought the cause was good and found it surprising that Georgia was involved in such things. Getting closer to when Stacy disappeared, Iris learned Georgia was pregnant with a child but had lost the baby early on, which explained the *March of Dimes* post. How sad to lose a child, Iris thought. She couldn't imagine how painful that must have been. But the curious thing was it didn't mention who the dad was. The only other thing of note was that Georgia had worked as an exotic dancer at a club called *Long Legs* before being recruited to work at *Southern Belles*. Wait a minute, why did that name sound familiar? Wondered Iris. She couldn't place it, but just then, her thoughts got interrupted by her phone ringing.

Seeing that it was her son, Iris answered the phone and said, "Good afternoon, Sammy. How are you doing?"

"Good afternoon, mom. I'm doing well. I just wanted to check to see how things are going. How was Barbados?"

After hesitating momentarily, Iris said, "Well, I can say without a doubt that someone has murdered Charles now."

"Oh, really? Why is that?"

"Well…" began Iris before continuing, "Someone pushed me into the street right as my taxi pulled up. But don't worry, I'm okay. The taxi stopped before hitting me."

"That's awful. You could have gotten seriously hurt or even killed. You need to stay out of this from now on because next time, you might not get so lucky."

"I know, Sammy. But it means I'm on the right trail. Otherwise, why would they try to harm me? If it makes you feel better, the captain informed me that a detective will come aboard to conduct an official investigation."

"That sounds promising. You need to leave this to the professionals. You're not Jessica Fletcher or Miss Marple, mom. This is real life, and you could get hurt or killed if you keep trying to play detective. Think about how sad Stella, her kids, and the rest of the family would be if something happened to you."

"I know, son. I will try to leave it to the professionals, then."

"Thanks, Mom. I hope you do. But I've got to go now. I got a date to get ready for."

"Wait, that reminds me. Before you go, I forgot to tell you I got a cute boy's number for you if you're interested."

"Mom, what did I tell you about meddling in my love life?"

"I know. But he's your type. A light blonde, skinny, big personality. And I told him it was up to you to reach out."

"Fair enough. I guess you can send me the name and number, and I'll consider it. But I'll probably decline. As I mentioned, I'm already seeing someone, and if things go well, I might ask him to be my boyfriend since this will be our fourth date."

"I understand, Sammy. I'll let you go then. Good luck with your date. I want all the details tomorrow."

Samuel laughed as he replied, "Thanks, Mom. I'll talk to you later," before hanging up.

Afterward, Iris got ready for dinner.

55

Present Day
Sunday, August 11, 2024, 6:00 p.m.

Iris entered the Soul Food restaurant on deck eight and was immediately hit with the smells of fried chicken, kale greens with a hint of vinegar, and fresh cornbread—all the comforts of a home-style southern meal. The smell made her mouth water and her stomach growl in anticipation. After they talked, the hostess seated her at a table and handed her a menu.

A few moments later, her server arrived and took her order. Iris asked for a glass of sweet tea, fried chicken, and some cornbread. After taking her menu, the server went to place her order. Iris looked around to see if she saw any of her suspects, but she had no such luck. She considered doing some research but reminded herself that she was supposed to leave the investigation to the professionals. Iris tapped the table nervously as she waited for her order to arrive.

A short while later, her food and drink arrived, and she eagerly dug in. The chicken reminded her of her Aunt Amelia's fried chicken growing up. And the cornbread was soft and buttery and melted in her mouth. She had to stop herself from eating too much. But in the end, her plate was empty, and her stomach was full. Iris felt a little sleepy as she got up and returned to her cabin.

As she entered her room, Iris sat down on her couch and closed her eyes. A quick nap sounded good to her. But a short while later, Iris jolted up as she heard someone knocking on her door. As she got up and headed towards the door, she said, "I'm coming."

As she opened the door, she saw a man dressed in a police uniform. Iris noticed that he also had a name tag that read Arabz on it as he said, "Good evening, Madame. My name is Inspector Arabz, and I'm here to ask you a few questions. May I come inside?"

"Of course, Inspector. Please come in," Iris replied as she opened the door and stepped aside.

"Thank you," murmured the Inspector as he walked inside her cabin. "This should only take a few minutes. I wanted to ask you some questions about Charles Underwood."

Iris led the inspector to the kitchen and asked, "Can I get you something to drink?"

"No thanks. I'm good. Can you tell me how well you knew the victim?"

"I didn't know him personally, but my late husband was the lead detective on his missing wife's case ten years ago. But it was never solved."

"I see. Did your husband suspect Charles was involved in his wife's disappearance?"

"Yes, he did, but Henry was unable to produce evidence, leaving the case unsolved."

"Did that make your husband resentful for being unable to solve that high-profile case?"

"It bothered him a little," admitted Iris as she continued, "But he learned to move past it."

"I see. So, you wouldn't have felt compelled to carry out your late husband's wishes to punish Charles since he was too powerful to convict? For example, drugging him and pushing his body into the pool late Friday night."

Iris looked shocked as she replied, "Of course not. I can't believe you think I led Charles up to the pool in the middle of the night, somehow got him to drink a drugged scotch bottle, and then pushed him into the pool. That's crazy!"

"Crazier things have happened. I have to ask since you have a connection with the victim, and you found the body."

"That's fair, I suppose. But there are several other people with stronger motives than me. You should talk to Nora Brooks, Selina Lagman, and Georgia Fisher. They all have past connections to Charles as well. Plus, someone dressed in a big floppy sun hat, sunglasses, and a scarf tried to push me in front of my taxi in Barbados today. And I think it's highly likely that one of them did it."

"That is very curious indeed. But can you prove you were, in fact, pushed into the street?"

"Ask my taxi driver. He can tell you. I should have a receipt for the ride." Iris got up and retrieved her purse before continuing, "Let me try to find it... here you go," as she handed the receipt to the Inspector.

After glancing at it, he carefully placed it into a zip-lock bag before putting it in his pocket. Then he said, "Thanks, I will investigate the matter. You have been very helpful, Madame. I will take my leave now."

"No problem," replied Iris as she watched the inspector walk away. Afterward, she locked her door and headed to her room to unwind for the night.

56

Present Day
Monday, August 12, 2024, 8:00 a.m.

Iris walked down a narrow pathway in the woods in the dark, following a glowing ball of light. No matter how fast she walked, the ball stood the same distance away from her. After what felt like an eternity, the orb of light stopped, and Iris caught up. The ball floated over a small garden of yellow flowers and slowly stopped in the center of the flowers. Then, a giant blinding light appeared, and Iris had to shield her eyes from the sight of it. A moment later, she heard her husband's voice say, "Watch out for the yellow carnation. It is a beautiful and captivating sight, but beneath the surface, it warns of rejection and disappointment. Remember, my love, that not all that glitters is gold."

"What are you trying to tell me, my love?"

Henry's voice slowly faded into the distance as he said, "Trust your gut. It won't let you down."

Just then, Iris heard her alarm go off, and her eyes slowly opened. As she reached to turn it off, she wondered what it all meant as she slowly got out of bed and got ready for the day.

After showering, Iris went to the kitchen and started a fresh pot of coffee. While she waited for it to brew, she searched for her event itinerary. Locating it, Iris flipped through to find today's activities. The only one of interest to her was a karaoke night that took place after dinner at 7:30 p.m., so she made a mental note before closing it and going to check on her coffee. It was finished, so she poured herself a cup and sat on the sofa. She sat there sipping her coffee and tried to plot out her goals for the day. Iris reasoned that she needed to question Sandy about finding his business card yesterday at the sight of her attack. Maybe she could see if anyone on board had potentially hired him for a job. Besides that, she also needed to find out where her other suspects were at the time of her attack, even if she learned little from it. Just then, Iris's stomach growled, and she laughed, saying, "I guess I need to eat some breakfast." After getting up from the sofa, she placed her coffee cup on the bar before going to fetch her purse from her room. Once retrieving it, she went out the front door, towards deck seven, in search of a cafe.

Once inside the cafe, Iris spotted Sandy standing at the checkout counter. What good fortune, she thought as she got in line. After placing her order, Iris scanned the room to locate Sandy. She found him eating a breakfast sandwich in the corner. She hoped she would have time to talk to him before he left. Thankfully, her food arrived shortly after. After paying, Iris approached Sandy and said, "Good morning, Sandy. Would it be okay for me to join you for a moment?"

Sandy looked uncertain as he said, "I guess, although I'm nearly finished with my breakfast."

"That's okay. I won't take up much of your time."

Sandy signaled Iris to sit, and he said, "All right. I can spare a few minutes."

Iris smiled as she sat down and said, "I appreciate it. I saw you and Nora having lunch yesterday in Barbados. I didn't know you two knew each other."

"Oh, we don't, really. The two of us met on this cruise

and got friendly. I'm sure you're wondering why I would be interested in a woman twenty years older than me."

"Not really," began Iris as she sipped her coffee, "I don't judge people. Besides, I think I might know why you would be interested in her."

Sandy looked amused as he replied, "Oh really? What do you think that is then?"

"Well, if I had to guess, I would either say she is one of your clients or someone paid you to shadow her."

Sandy looked dumbfounded as he asked, "How do you know that?"

Iris took a bite of her muffin before replying, "I found one of your business cards yesterday. So, it was an educated guess."

"How did you locate one of my business cards in Barbados, of all places?"

"Funny you should ask that. I found it on the ground after someone tried to push me in front of my taxi. Where were you at around 3:30 p.m. yesterday?"

Sandy looked bewildered as he said, "I was at Carlisle Bay with Nora. So, it wasn't either of us. As for why someone would have one of my business cards, I couldn't say. How peculiar!"

Iris wasn't sure if he was lying, so she said, "Quite peculiar. But back to you being hired. Did Nora hire you, or are you spying on her?"

Sandy appeared uncomfortable as he said, "I'm not at liberty to say due to client confidentiality."

"Fair enough, I suppose. I hope nobody else ends up dead because of your silence."

Sandy looked pale as he said, "I hope so, too. Anyway, I need to get going." He stood, picked up his trash, and said, "Take care, Iris," before hurrying off.

Iris sat contemplating what he'd just said. As she finished her breakfast, she still wasn't sure if he was involved in her attack. After getting up and throwing away her trash, Iris considered where to go next.

57

Present Day
Monday, August 12, 2024, 9:15 a.m.

Since Iris was right by the library, she thought now would be a good time to do more research. So, she made her way over there. Once inside, Iris walked to the back, where the computers were located. After sitting down, she opened *Google* and searched for Sandy's background. As she clicked on his website, she noticed several anonymous positive reviews that spoke highly of Sandy's work as a private investigator. But from the look of things, most were cheating spouses or missing person cases. Iris laughed at the irony of these statements supporting the private investigator stereotype. But it made her wonder what Sandy was hired to do on the cruise. Maybe Nora had hired Sandy to watch Charles, but that seems odd since Charles was dead, and Nora seemed shocked to see Charles at dinner Friday night. So that didn't seem right. The only other option was if he was spying on Nora or if she had hired him to spy on someone else on the cruise. But if so, who? Iris couldn't figure it out. So, she looked at the website more but found nothing of interest.

Switching to his social media, Iris noticed Sandy posted several photos of him at theme parks, rock climbing, and zip lining. Seems like he was a thrill seeker, Iris mused as she continued to look through his *Facebook*. However, nothing else of interest stood out to her. So, she switched over to look at Nora's stuff again, but before hitting enter, she heard Nora's voice call to her in the distance.

"What are you up to, Iris?"

"I'm just checking some emails," Iris lied as she continued. "The Wi-Fi on the ship is hit or miss, and this is the best spot to get a signal."

"That makes sense. I've had trouble checking my social media the last few days on the ship, which can be frustrating sometimes."

"I bet it is for someone with your kind of job. But on a side note, I was wondering if the inspector has come and questioned you about Charles's death yet?"

"It is. But I can function without the internet too, so that you know. But it's funny you should mention that he came and questioned me last night. He wanted to know about my connection to Charles Underwood. How about you, Iris? Did he come and ask you about his death?"

"Yes, he did as well. Although I had little to tell him."

Nora looked skeptical as she said, "Same here. But I would have thought you would have more to say since you found the body. But regardless, I wonder what really happened to him."

Iris blushed slightly as she said, "Yeah, but there wasn't much to tell. He was face down in the pool. But it seemed odd somehow. The police seem to think so. That means someone on the ship must be under suspicion then."

Nora turned pale as she said, "That's a scary thought to think about. Anyway, I'll leave you alone now. I have some research to do."

Iris smiled as she said, "Before you go, I want to ask you a question."

Nora looked intrigued as she said, "Ask away. Now I'm curious."

"What were you doing around 3:30 p.m. yesterday?"

Nora looked surprised and said, "Well, I can't remember. I think Sandy and I were shopping in town. Otherwise, we were in Carlisle Bay scuba diving. Why are you asking?"

"Well, around that time, someone tried to push me in front of my taxi. So, I'm trying to figure out who did it."

Shock covered Nora's face as she said, "That's horrible. I'm glad you weren't hurt. But it wasn't Sandy or I, if that's what you think. Besides, what motive would we have?"

"You both seemed to have a strong response when I told you Charles had died. So, it stands to reason that both of you might have a reason to kill him, and since I have been asking about him, one of you might have seen me as a threat to be removed."

Nora looked horrified as she said, "That's awful to think we did such a thing, and with no proof to boot. Anyway, I need to get going now. Bye," then Nora turned around and went down one aisle.

How peculiar, thought Iris. She could understand why Nora was upset, but the facts were someone on the ship most likely had tried to kill her, and if it wasn't them, then one of her other suspects was to blame. Iris thought she needed a brief break from sleuthing. A little dip in the pool sounded nice, so she got up and headed to her room to change.

58

Present Day
Monday, August 12, 2024, 10:00 a.m.

In her cabin, Iris changed into her bathing suit, grabbed a beach towel and her novel from her nightstand before locating her purse and heading out the door. Then she made her way to the pool.

As Iris strolled past the pool and settled on the lounge chairs on deck nine, the potent scent of chlorine filled her senses. She laid her beach towel on the chair, opened her novel, and began reading. Her attention was quickly drawn to familiar voices in the distance. Iris peered over her book and spotted Jordan and Selina engaged in a conversation. A thought crossed her mind: Now was the perfect time to inquire about their alibis. She set her book aside, rose from her chair, and approached the couple, her heart pounding with anticipation.

As she approached the couple, Selina turned and saw Iris. She was wearing a bright yellow bikini, her blonde hair pulled back into a messy bun. She gave a disappointed look before quickly turning into a smile and saying, "Oh, hi there, Iris. How are you doing?"

Iris smiled before saying, "I'm doing all right. I was just lying out and reading my book when I heard you guys talking. I was just wondering if the Inspector questioned you about Charles's death or not."

Selina looked nervous as she said, "Yes, he had. But unfortunately, we had little to tell him." Then she looked at Jordan before continuing, "Right, babe?"

Jordan looked up from the pool and said, "That's right. We told him we hadn't seen Charles in years, so we didn't help him much."

"You said we. Does that mean you knew Charles in the past, then, Jordan?"

Jordan hesitated for a moment before saying, "No, not really. Just what Selina told me about her dealings with her mom's death."

"I see," Iris began before continuing, "On a side note, I was wondering where you guys were yesterday at 3:30 p.m.?"

The couple looked surprised as Selina said, "We were shopping in Bridgetown. Why do you want to know?"

"Well, someone tried to push me in front of my taxi," Iris revealed, her voice tinged with a hint of mystery.

Jordan looked angry as he said, "Well, it wasn't us if that's what you're implying." His face was flushed, and his voice was tense with anger.

Iris spoke innocently, saying, "No, of course not. I was just wondering. Anyway, I won't bother you anymore," before leaving. As she walked away, she couldn't help but feel a nagging suspicion. Something about their alibis and reactions didn't quite add up. She needed to find more information.

While doing so, she heard the couple muttering a clipped "Goodbye" as she returned to her lounge chair.

SEVERAL HOURS LATER, IRIS STOOD OUTSIDE HER ROOM, searching for her key card. The hallway was dimly lit, and a faint scent of sea salt filled the air. After rummaging through her bag for a few minutes, she found it. After unlocking the door, Iris returned her key and zipped up her bag before entering her cabin.

Once inside, she changed out of her bathing suit. Afterward, she returned her book to her nightstand. Then she ordered room service. While she waited, Iris turned on the TV in her bedroom. The movie *Vertigo* popped on the screen. Iris sat on the bed and relaxed as she watched the familiar film while waiting for her lunch to arrive.

A short while later, Iris heard a knock on the door. She grabbed the remote and paused the movie as she went to answer the door. When she opened the door, Iris saw Joanne standing next to a cart with a silver platter, much like the one she had received the other day for breakfast. Joanne smiled as she said, "Room service for Iris May."

"That's me," replied Iris eagerly.

"Good to see you again, Iris. I hope everything turned out well the last time."

Iris nodded.

"Glad to hear it," replied Joanne as she retrieved the receipt from her pocket along with a pen and said, "Please just sign the tab, and you'll be good to go."

"Will do," Iris replied as she signed the dotted line.

"Thanks, Miss. Here's your lunch," she said, handing Iris the platter.

"Thanks so much," replied Iris, taking the platter before returning to her cabin.

Iris savored her chicken Caesar salad. Each bite was a delightful blend of creamy dressing, fresh romaine lettuce, and sprinkles of parmesan cheese. As the movie's credits rolled, she relished the last bite of her salad, feeling thoroughly satisfied. Delicious, she thought, turning off the TV and heading to the sink to clean up. Afterward, she returned to her bedroom and enjoyed a peaceful nap before dinner.

59

Present Day
Monday, August 12, 2024, 5:00 p.m.

Iris woke up and checked the time on her phone. It read 5:00 p.m. It was time to get ready for dinner, she thought. So, she stretched and got out of bed. Then she went to the bathroom to brush her hair and apply some makeup. When finished, she picked up her purse before heading out the door.

As Iris entered the Japanese restaurant on deck eight, the smell of fresh fish mixed with a hint of seaweed immediately took her in. It brought back memories of walking down the beach and smelling the fresh sea air—just the smell one would expect from a high-class Japanese restaurant. After talking to the host, the host seated her at a table and handed her a menu.

Iris glanced at the menu. After some consideration, she settled on seafood ramen and a California roll with a glass of water. A few moments later, the server arrived and took her order.

While she waited, Iris scanned the room to see if she had

spotted any of her suspects. But had no luck. That was the second time in a row. So, she thought she might as well try to do some research to kill some time until her food arrived. Since she hadn't got to look up Nora again, Iris did that. As she went through Nora's *Instagram*, she saw a lot of photos of her scuba diving, snorkeling, and other aqua activities at different locations back in Orlando. She also noticed that Nora was a wiz with a camera since she took breathtaking photos of various nature scenes. But that shouldn't be too surprising since she was a reporter, mused Iris. But the thought reminded Iris that Stacy Underwood had also been a reporter. Iris wondered if there was a connection. So, she tried looking up Stacy Underwood's old accounts, but her food arrived just as it was loading. Guess it would have to wait, mused Iris as she put her phone away and ate.

A short while later, Iris wiped her mouth with her napkin as she stared at the empty bowl, plate, and glass before her. The meal had been divine, with the perfect amount of sweetness and saltiness between the two dishes. She hadn't had authentic Japanese food like that in a long time. It was such a treat! A few moments later, after paying the check, Iris got up to leave, but while doing so, the intercom came on and said, "Good evening, everyone. I hope you're doing well. This is your captain speaking. I have two announcements to make. The first is that karaoke night will begin at 7:30 p.m. on deck nine at the same location as the trivia night was located. The second message is that we will arrive in St. Lucia tomorrow at 9:00 a.m. So, make sure you are up and ready tomorrow morning. As before, ensure you are present for the ship's departure tomorrow at 5 p.m., as we will not pick up or provide a refund for anyone who misses it. So please keep that in mind. Other than that, I hope everyone has a good day on the SS Paradise."

Iris smiled as she thought it was time to go get ready for the karaoke night. As she headed back to her room eagerly.

60

Present Day
Monday, August 12, 2024, 7:20 p.m.

Iris entered deck nine and headed to the lounge area. Once there, she saw a line of people, which she assumed was for karaoke night. As she got closer, she saw a staff member holding a clipboard and talking to someone at the front of the line. This strengthened her assumption as she got in line and waited her turn.

A short while later, Iris stood at the front of the line. The staff member, whose name tag read Oliver, looked at her and asked, "What is your name?"

"Iris May," replied Iris eagerly as she watched the man write something on his clipboard.

"How many people are in your group? And what song will you be singing?"

Iris thought momentarily, debating what song she should sing before saying, "Just one person. And I think I'll go with *Every Breath You Take* by *The Police*."

Oliver made more notes on his clipboard before saying, "Sounds good. Please take a seat. We'll be starting shortly."

"Will do," Iris replied as she stepped out of line and went to find an available chair. After a few moments, she located one and sat down. As she waited for the event to begin, Iris looked around to see if any of her suspects were around. As she glanced through the crowd, she spotted Nora and Sandy sitting beside each other, chatting far from her seat. She also spotted Jordan and Selina doing the same thing in another section of the lounge. Next to them also sat Tyler and Georgia, lost in conversation.

A few moments later, Oliver returned with two microphones in one hand, a clipboard under one arm, and pulling the jukebox with the other. The sound of the jukebox wheels rolling on the floor filled the air. After placing the microphones and clipboard on a lounge chair, he set the jukebox on the floor. Then he cleared his throat and addressed the group by saying, "Good evening, and welcome to the SS Paradise's karaoke night. My name is Oliver, and I'll be your host tonight. Before we get started, here are some ground rules for the karaoke night. Each person gets a turn to sing a song of their choice. Then, after everyone has had a turn, we'll open the floor for anyone to pick a song. Sound good, everyone?"

The entire group said, "Yes," in unison.

Oliver replied, "All right," as he picked up his clipboard and said, "First up is Jordan and Selina singing *Islands in the Stream* by Kenny Rogers and Dolly Parton."

Oliver picked up the two microphones off the lounge chair and turned them on before handing them to Jordan and Selina. Then he turned on the jukebox and started the song. A moment later, the opening of *Islands in the Stream* played. Shortly after, the music began, and Selina and Jordan started singing. Not surprisingly, neither sounded great, Iris thought, but both seemed to enjoy themselves as they sang together, and that image made her smile. It reminded Iris of her and Henry when they were young and in their 20s. She could tell that the young couple loved each other very much as the song ended.

Afterward, the couple returned the microphones as the

group clapped for their performance. A moment later, Oliver said, "Nice job, you two," before looking at his clipboard and saying, "Next up is…"

Iris listened to several other people sing their songs until finally she heard Oliver say, "Next up is Georgia singing *Queens Don't* by RaeLynn."

Iris then watched Oliver hand Georgia the microphone before starting up the song. A moment later, Georgia started singing, surprising Iris with how good she was. Iris watched as Georgia's performance entranced several members of the crowd.

After Georgia finished, Tyler sang *Blank Space* by Tayler Swift. Interesting choice, Iris thought as the song played. Tyler also had a surprisingly pleasant voice as he sang.

After listening to several other performances, Iris's attention was piqued when she heard Oliver announce, "Next up is Nora singing *Jolene* by Dolly Parton." Iris was intrigued by Nora's song choice, but what really caught her attention was Nora's occasional glances in Georgia's direction. Iris couldn't help but wonder what was going on between them as the song ended.

Next up was Sandy, who sang *Don't Stop Believing* by *Journey*. Iris thought it was such a classic as Sandy sang in an offbeat tone. She also noticed that Nora sang along with him towards the end of the song and that they were both grinning ear to ear. Iris thought they both seemed to get rather close as the song ended.

After Sandy finished, he returned the microphone. Then Oliver said, "Good job on a classic, Sandy." Then he checked his clipboard and said, "Next up is Iris singing *Every Breath You Take* by *The Police*."

A moment later, Oliver handed Iris the microphone before starting the music. As the familiar tune of *Every Breath You Take* filled the room, Iris's heart raced. She knew time was running out and was determined to uncover the truth before the cruise ended. She was not just singing a song; she was making a vow to herself to get justice for Charles and finally close her late husband's cold case.

After the song ended, Iris returned the microphone to Oliver. A moment later, he said, "Nice job, Iris. Now, it's time for the next song…" After the last few people finished singing, Oliver said, "Now that everyone has had a turn, it's time to open up the floor for anyone to play. Otherwise, you're free to go. But please remember that we will land in St. Lucia tomorrow morning."

Iris noticed that Tyler and Georgia had gotten up and headed to the bar. Shortly afterward, she saw Nora and Sandy exit the lounge area along with several others, leaving Selina, Jordan, and a few others to sing some freestyle songs. Iris thought it was time to leave. As she headed out, she heard Jordan and Selina singing *I Got You, Babe*, by Sonny and Cher. How cute, Iris thought. But as she exited the lounge, she spotted Inspector Arabz standing in the corner, observing the couple sing. She wondered if he had been there watching all of them singing the whole time or if he had just got there and entered the bar.

Once inside the bar, Iris noticed Tyler getting up from the bar and coming over to her and saying, "Sorry to bother you, Iris, but I was wondering if you gave my number to your son yet? I was talking to Georgia about it, and she wanted to see a picture of him and wanted to know if he was interested in me."

Iris felt a pang of guilt as she said, "Sorry, Tyler, but I told my son Samuel, and he said he just started dating somebody. Otherwise, he would have reached out." She could see the disappointment in Tyler's eyes, but he quickly masked it with a smile.

Tyler's disappointment was fleeting, quickly replaced by a warm smile. "No worries. I understand, girlfriend. I hope things work out for him. I'll leave you alone then and go back to Georgia," he said, his voice filled with genuine understanding and kindness.

Iris felt a twinge of sadness, but Tyler's quick recovery was evident in the way he effortlessly rejoined Georgia at the bar. The sound of laughter and music filled the air, and the warm glow of the bar's lights added to the cheerful atmosphere. It was nice of him to wish her son good luck. She hoped both of them would find happiness as she headed back to her cabin, the night air cool against her skin.

61

Present Day
Monday, August 12, 2024, 8:45 p.m.

As Iris entered her cabin, her phone rang. After closing the door, she pulled out her phone and saw Stella was calling her; as she hit answer a moment later, she heard Stella say, "Good evening, Mom. How was Barbados the other day?"

Iris remembered not to mention anything about Charles's death or her attack as she said, "Good evening, Stel. It was really nice. I got to see a fascinating old church and a rum pub before I went shopping. How are you doing?"

"That sounds like fun. I'm doing well. I just gave the kids their baths and tucked them in a minute ago, so now I'm unwinding before bed. How about you, Mom?"

"Same. I just returned from karaoke night and plan to relax before bed. We land in St. Lucia tomorrow morning."

"Karaoke night sounds like fun. Did you enjoy yourself?"

"Yeah, it was fun. There were even a few talented singers, too."

Stella laughed and said, "I'm glad to hear you enjoyed

yourself. But I won't keep you. I know you got to get up early tomorrow."

"Thanks, Stel. Goodnight, please tell my grandbabies I love them."

Iris heard Stella say, "I will. Goodnight, Mom," before hanging up the phone. Afterward, she went into her bedroom, lay on her bed, and turned on the TV as she unwound for the night.

62

Present Day
Monday, August 12, 2024, Time Unknown

Sandy was sitting at the bar in his cabin. He was reviewing the case file Charles gave him over a week ago. He was trying to figure out why Charles had hired him to investigate Nora when he got on the boat himself. Sandy had worked with paranoid clients before, but Charles didn't even try to hide his presence from Sandy on the cruise. But a knock on his door interrupted his thoughts. Sandy wondered who that could be as he went to answer the door. He had already dropped Nora off earlier after karaoke night. But that had been quite some time ago. He wondered if she needed something as he opened the door.

Outside the door stood a figure shrouded in mystery. Sandy couldn't quite place the face, yet it stirred a sense of familiarity. How peculiar, he mused, as the person uttered, "Hello, there. Are you Sandy Stone, the private investigator?"

Taken aback by this stranger who somehow knew he was a private eye. His heart raced, but he maintained his composure. Curiosity got the better of him, so he said, "That's right, but how do you know that?"

The stranger laughed dramatically before saying, "My bad, I just thought I recognized you, so I looked you up online and thought you matched the guy whose picture popped up. Anyway, I guess I have some information that might interest you regarding Charles Underwood if you let me come inside and explain."

This unexpected turn of events piqued Sandy's curiosity. He was still in the dark about the stranger's identity and the nature of their information, but one thing was certain: Sandy was eager to uncover the truth. With a nod, he opened the door and said, "Sure, come on in."

So, the stranger followed suit and entered Sandy's cabin. A moment later, the stranger said, "Do you care if we discuss this over a drink?"

Sandy thought this might get his mysterious guest to open up more. So, he said, "Sure thing. Follow me into the kitchen, and let's see what I have."

Once inside, Sandy opened the minibar and said, "It looks like I got some wine, vodka, beer, and scotch."

"Scotch works for me."

"Sounds good to me," replied Sandy as he took the bottle out of the mini fridge and placed it on the bar before continuing, "Give me a minute to find some glasses."

"Take your time," replied his guest.

After locating some glasses, Sandy returned to the bar and poured some into both glasses. As he went to hand one to his guest, his guest interrupted him, saying, "Sorry, but can you put some ice into my drink?"

Sandy smiled and replied, "Sure thing," before grabbing the glass. Then Sandy went to put some ice in it. After returning to the table, he handed his guest the glass before saying, "There you go. Now, can you please tell me the information you have?"

The guest smiled like a cat before saying, "Of course. But first, let's have a toast."

Sandy's patience was wearing thin. But he played along for now. He raised his glass and said, "Cheers," before taking a sip. Yet, in that moment, something felt off. Sandy's vision blurred, and a sense of unease washed over him. As he fought against the encroaching darkness, he finally recognized his guest.

63

Present Day
Tuesday, August 13, 2024, 7:15 a.m.

As Iris's alarm went off, she stretched and turned it off before getting ready for the day. After grabbing some fresh clothes, she headed to the shower. Once she finished, she brushed her teeth and headed to the kitchen to look for the ship's itinerary.

After locating it, she searched for the room service number. A few moments later, she located it. Iris added the number to her phone's contact list in case she needed it during the rest of the trip before calling it. A few rings later, Joanne greeted her and said, "Good morning, Hun. What can I get for you this morning?"

"I would like to order biscuits and gravy with a side of sausage, please, Joanne."

"Sure thing, Miss. That will be about a twenty-five-minute wait. Is that acceptable?"

"Yes, that's fine. Please place my order."

Joanne replied cheerfully, "Certainly, Miss. I'll bring your food shortly," she said before hanging up the phone.

Afterward, Iris went and started a pot of fresh coffee to have with her upcoming breakfast. As she waited for it to brew, Iris returned to the itinerary to check out what St. Lucia had to offer today. After locating the right page, she saw that the most famous attraction on the island was called *The Pitons*, which are two mountains that house volcanos with breathtaking sights. Considering her close encounter with danger in Barbados, this seemed interesting but perhaps a little dangerous. So, Iris continued looking. According to the itinerary, *Sulfur Springs* was the second most popular tourist site. They were located in the town of Soufriere, which is home to the Caribbean's only drive-in volcano. That seemed interesting. But as she continued reading, the pamphlet said that *Sulphur Springs* also housed bubbling mud pools created from Sulphur steam from the ground. That also seemed potentially dangerous. So, Iris kept on looking. After considering many other choices, she finally found something safe. The bottom of the page listed *Anse Chastanet Beach*, which housed shallow reefs to explore. That seemed scenic and safe since she didn't plan on going snorkeling. The beach sounded like a good way to relax and get some reading done today. Iris smiled at her choice as she heard a knock on her door.

After paying for her food, Iris returned with her platter and sat it on the bar. Then she went to check on her coffee. The coffee had finished brewing, so she retrieved a cup from the cabinet, poured herself some coffee, and then returned to the bar to eat her breakfast.

Despite the chaos and potential dangers she was in, Iris was sure that one highlight of this trip was the food. Breakfast had been scrumptious. The biscuits were light and flakey, while the gravy was creamy and thick. In addition, they cooked the sausage to perfection. She almost didn't care about the cost since the food was five-star. The joy of indulging in such a delicious meal filled her heart, reminding her of the simple pleasures in life. But Iris realized she had lost track of time. So, she checked the time. Her phone read 8:30 a.m. It was getting late; the ship would land in port in half an hour, and she needed to grab her stuff. So, she got up and retrieved everything she needed for the day before heading to the bridge, a sense of urgency and excitement propelling her forward.

On the bridge, Iris spotted Tyler and Georgia chatting together like usual. She wondered where they were going today. It also made her wonder where her other suspects were going. So, she scanned the bridge to see if she could spot any of them. She spotted Jordan and Selina standing close together on the opposite side of where Tyler and Georgia were located. But still no sight of Nora or Sandy. A few moments later, the captain announced they were about to land. Iris wondered if she would run into Nora or Sandy as the ship landed at the St. Lucia pier.

64

Present Day
Tuesday, August 13, 2024, 9:00 a.m.

As Iris walked down the gangplank into St. Lucia, she kept an eye out for her two missing suspects to no avail. Like last time, the pier smelled salty, but this time, it also mixed with a fresh, earthy scent you sometimes get after a rainstorm. The combined effect was surprisingly appealing. She also saw several ships in port, like the last time she had walked down the pier.

At the end of the pier, Iris spotted Nora alone, engrossed in a phone conversation. The absence of Sandy, her usual companion as of late, was a stark contrast. Iris couldn't help but wonder if a rift had formed between the two. As she approached, she caught a snippet of Nora's conversation, "I love you too," before the call abruptly ended. The mystery deepened. Who was Nora talking to? Nora, startled by Iris's presence, greeted her casually, "Oh, hi there, Iris. I didn't see you there. How are you doing?"

Iris smiled as she said, "I'm doing well. I wondered if you were doing all right since I didn't spot Sandy with you. I wondered if you two had gotten into a fight since you seemed to get close recently."

Nora blushed slightly as she said, "Oh, how sweet of you to ask. No, we didn't have a fight. Although…" Nora stopped momentarily before continuing in a concerned tone, "I am slightly worried about him. I saw he had his *Do Not Disturb* sign hanging on his door this morning."

That seemed odd to Iris as she said, "I can see why you're worried, but he's probably all right. Maybe he just got a little seasick or had too much to drink last night."

"You're probably right. I just got this nagging feeling something is off. But I'm probably just overacting since this whole Charles thing happened this week."

"It has been a stressful week for sure. I'm sure Sandy is fine, and it's just nerves you're worrying over. Anyway, where are you headed today?"

"I completely forgot. I called a taxi a moment ago before you arrived to go to *Anse Chastanet Beach*. It should arrive any minute."

How interesting, Iris thought. She was pretty sure Nora hadn't been talking to the taxi driver before she arrived. But why would Nora lie about that? Unless Nora had called for a taxi before Iris arrived. But if that was the case, Iris wondered whom she was talking to. But before she got the chance, the taxi arrived, and Nora said, "Here it is now," before getting in the taxi.

Iris thought she would have to ask Nora about the phone call later. It was too bad she couldn't join Nora in the taxi. Maybe she would run into Nora again later at the beach. But for now, she pulled out her phone and looked up a taxi service. After finding one, Iris called and gave the service her location before hanging up. Then she sat on the bench while waiting for the taxi to arrive.

A short while later, the taxi arrived, and Iris got in. After buckling up, the driver asked, "Where are we headed?"

"I would like to go to *Anse Chastanet Beach*, please."

"That's a bit of a drive, Miss. It's going to cost a bundle. Are you sure you still want to go there?"

"Yes, I'm sure."

The taxi driver replied, "Okay, I just wanted to warn you before we took off."

"I appreciate the warning, but I still want to go."

"All right then, Miss. To *Anse Chastanet Beach* then." Then, a few moments later, the taxi driver turned on some soothing local music as they drove to their destination.

65

Present Day
Tuesday, August 13, 2024, 11:00 a.m.

After parking the taxi, Iris paid her fare before exiting the vehicle. She took her first look at *Anse Chastanet Beach* as it drove away. Like most tropical beaches, it housed a quarter of a mile of light-colored sand lined with palm trees that were haphazardly scattered about it. To wrap up the scene, a few radios played different kinds of music across the beach, and hordes of beach towels were laid out with some people lying on them. In contrast, some people recklessly abandoned their beach towels without care while they either built sandcastles, swam in the crystal-clear water, or snorkeled below the surface. The entire scene gave Iris a wholesome feeling.

Walking across the sand, Iris searched for a free spot to lie down on her beach towel. But unfortunately, there didn't seem to be a spot in sight. Walking farther down the beach, Iris spotted Selina and Jordan dressed in swimming attire. What were the odds of running into them? Iris mused as she got closer to the couple. But as she walked past them, she noticed Jordan was wearing a sleeveless T-shirt, which wasn't all that interesting. But since it was sleeveless, Iris saw the chest binder underneath the shirt, which only meant one thing. Jordan must be trans. Not that the revelation was a shock to Iris; she had a few family members and friends who identified as trans or non-binary. But it changed things a little bit. If Jordan was trans and still wore a chest binder, then it was quite possible for him to disguise himself as a woman and try to push her in Barbados. She would have to look further into his background and see what she could find out. But if she had overlooked Jordan's suspicion, she also needed to reevaluate her thoughts on Tyler and Sandy. Tyler had a background in a makeup company and could easily have the skills to know how to alter his appearance. As for Sandy, she had found his business card at the crime scene. Plus, being a private eye meant Sandy might also have the skills to alter his appearance. Iris felt foolish for dismissing such thoughts earlier. That meant any of her suspects could have tried and pushed her. She would have to review her notes later to see if she overlooked anything else. But for now, she still needed to locate a place to lie down on her beach towel so she could relax.

A few moments later, Iris found an ideal spot open up. It was in a shady spot off to the side of the beach. A perfect place to read, Iris thought as she opened her bag and pulled out her fold-up beach towel. After unfolding it, Iris placed it on the ground. Then, she grabbed her book and got comfortable. One of her goals today was to finish her book. So, Iris eagerly laid down on her beach towel and began to read.

66

Present Day
Tuesday, August 13, 2024, 1:00 p.m.

Deeply engrossed in reading, her concentration broke as she suddenly heard her stomach growl. Iris laughed as she thought she should get some lunch. After placing her bookmark in her book to save her progress, she closed it and placed it in her bag. Then she picked up her beach towel and gave it a shake to get off any sand before rolling it up and placing it in her bag as well. Afterward, she pulled out her phone and saw the time. Iris couldn't believe how late it had gotten as she pulled up *Google* and searched for a place to have lunch. Luckily, there was a place within walking distance. As she clicked the directions, *Google Maps* popped up, leading her to her destination.

A short while later, Iris stood outside a small restaurant called *She Sails*. How cute, she thought as she entered the building. After getting seated, Iris ordered a glass of sweet tea with clam chowder and a side salad. While waiting for her lunch, Iris glanced around the restaurant to see if she recognized anyone. But unfortunately, none of her suspects were around. Iris's mind was buzzing with curiosity about what they were all up to today. She knew Nora was supposed to be scuba diving at the beach. She also ran into Jordan and Selina at the beach, although she wasn't sure what they were doing now. That reminded Iris that she still had many questions needing answers, and since she wasn't doing anything, now would be a good time to do some research. But the question was, who to focus on? After a moment of consideration, Iris started with Jordan since she had just learned about his trans status.

After loading up *Google* again, Iris tried to dive deeper into Jordan. So, as she scrolled through *Facebook*, Iris tried to locate anyone of interest who connected Jordan to Charles in any new way. She mainly saw pictures of him with Selina throughout the years and many people from their families. But finally, after scrolling for a while, Iris found something that stood out. She found a post from last year that talked about the anniversary of the death of Jordan's parents nine years ago, dated shortly after Stacy Underwood disappeared. Iris wondered if there was a connection as she scrolled farther down the timeline. But she got interrupted by the server, who returned with her drink and her food. So, Iris sat her phone down to focus on her lunch.

As Iris took the last bite of her clam chowder, she heard a notification on her phone. As she went to see what it was, she saw her son had updated his *Facebook* status to be in a relationship. Iris smiled as she clicked the notification and watched *Facebook* load onto her screen. A moment later, she saw the status read, *In a Relationship* with Ryan Sterling. After typing a quick congratulations message, Iris looked up Ryan's profile to see what her son's new boyfriend looked like. A picture of a chestnut-haired man wearing a nice suit and tie, stylish glasses, and a slight five o'clock shadow appeared on the screen. Iris thought the man looked handsome, but she worried he might be a playboy. So, she checked out his profile a little bit. But she relaxed as she saw he worked as a librarian and participated in various charity events. Iris felt a wave of relief, hoping her son finally found a good one this time. But before she could muse further, her server returned, and her focus shifted to paying the bill.

After the server returned with her receipt, Iris hurriedly exited the restaurant. As she got outside, she checked the time on her phone. It read, 2:20 p.m. It was getting late, and she had an hour-and-a-half drive back to the ship. So, Iris immediately called a taxi service to come pick her up. After a few rings, the service answered and said, "A car is on its way," before hanging up. So, Iris paced outside the restaurant, anxiously waiting for her ride to show up.

67

Present Day
Tuesday, August 13, 2024, 2:30 p.m.

As the taxi arrived, Iris stepped inside. After sitting down, she told the driver to take her back to the docks. A few moments later, the driver headed off to their destination.

On the way to the dock, Iris tried to do some more research while she still had stable Wi-Fi. She wanted to finish her research on Jordan. So, she hopped back on *Facebook* and scrolled down the timeline. Once she got closer to when Stacy disappeared, she discovered a post that showed the official start of Jordan and Selina's relationship. The interesting thing was it was posted a few weeks after Stacy had disappeared and Inga had been killed. Shortly before that, another post discussed how Jordan's parents died from complications because of a car accident. Iris found the timing to be very curious. Another interesting thing was that even further past, there was a post that stated that Jordan had worked as an intern at *Underwood Real Estate* back that summer. Iris wondered if that was how Jordan had met Selina through

Inga. She would have to ask him later when she got the chance. Unfortunately, she found nothing else of interest past that point.

Moving on, Iris switched gears and started looking further into Tyler's background. As she looked through his social media, she saw several photos of him and Georgia at various fashion events throughout the years. She also saw some advertisements Tyler had made for the company he worked for, *Doll Face*. They all looked very professional and colorful. Tyler must be good at his job, reasoned Iris as she continued her search. As she scrolled further down, Iris saw old exes of Tyler's throughout the years. All the men seemed to range from various ages and looks, but all seemed to be distinguished somehow. One was an actor, banker, and professional dancer. It seems like Tyler didn't really have a type. As she got closer to when Stacy disappeared, she saw something interesting. She found the post about Tyler's recruitment to work for *Doll Face*. The date listed was the fall of the year Stacy disappeared. This made her wonder if this was when he met Georgia. She would have to ask him later. Just as she was about to switch to another suspect, the taxi arrived at the port. After paying her fare, Iris exited the car and returned to the ship.

68

Present Day
Tuesday, August 13, 2024, 4:00 p.m.

As Iris walked down the hallway towards her room, she spotted the *Do Not Disturb* sign still hanging on Sandy's door. This alarmed her, so she approached the door and gently knocked on it, saying, "Sandy, it's Iris. Is everything all right?"

After a few moments of silence, Iris tried to pound on the door as she spoke more loudly, "Sandy, are you hurt? Please say something!"

Once again, silence. By this time, Iris panicked. Something was wrong. She could feel it in her gut. What to do? She wondered. But just then, an idea popped into her head. The captain had given her his phone number in case she needed to contact him. So, she pulled her phone out and called the captain. A few moments later, he picked up the phone and said, "Hello, whose number is this?"

Iris spoke frantically, "It's Iris. Captain Rivers. I'm calling because I think something might have happened to Sandy. He has had his *Do Not Disturb* sign on his cabin door all day, and when I tried to knock, he didn't answer. Can you please come and see if he's okay?"

"Sure thing. Thanks for letting me know. I'll be there in a few moments."

"Please hurry," replied Iris before she hung up the phone. Afterward, she paced back and forth while she waited for the captain to arrive.

About ten minutes later, Captain Rivers appeared. He approached the door and firmly knocked, shouting, "Sandy, this is Captain Rivers. I'm here to check on your well-being. If you don't reply, then I'm going to enter your cabin, okay?"

A few moments of silence ensued before the captain said, "Okay, Sandy, I'm coming inside." He withdrew his primary key, unlocked the door, and entered. But as soon as the door opened, the captain raised his arm as a shield and said, "Don't come in, Iris." However, Iris looked past him and saw Sandy lying on the floor in an unnatural position. Fear and pain covered her face as she stood in shock.

A moment later, Captain River bent down to check Sandy's pulse. But as he did so, Iris noticed he had accidentally dropped his master key, so she covertly bent down and retrieved it before quickly retreating to her original spot as the captain said, "He's dead. I'm going to have to call the Inspector. Can you please return to your cabin for now?"

Iris murmured, "Sure thing," as she left Sandy's room. Iris walked in a daze as she headed back to her room.

Once inside, Iris sat down at the bar, got out a bottle of wine, and poured herself a glass. She couldn't believe Sandy was dead. Despite not knowing him well, Iris still felt sad at the loss of a young life before his time. But that raised a question. If someone murdered Sandy, then how was he connected to Charles's death? Maybe someone hired Sandy to shadow someone, and that could be related. But it seemed unlikely Nora would have wanted to kill him. They seemed to be sweet on each other. Nora! Iris had completely forgotten. She had been upset about Sandy's absence this morning. Learning about Sandy's death would devastate her. Iris needed to comfort Nora somehow. The problem was that Iris was unclear when Nora would return to the ship or what cabin she was staying in. But an idea popped into her head. Iris withdrew her phone, called up room service, and put her plan into motion.

69

Present Day
Tuesday, August 13, 2024, 4:30 p.m.

Iris heard a knock on her door and sprang up with anticipation. She expected it to be Nora, but to her surprise, it was Inspector Arabz. He said, "Good afternoon, Madame. I'm here to question you about Sandy. May I please come inside?"

"Sure thing, Inspector. Please come in. Although I'm not sure how much help I can be," Iris replied, her voice tinged with a hint of suspicion.

Inspector Arabz replied, "I'm sure you know a lot more than you think," as he entered the cabin.

This comment caused Iris to blush as she led the Inspector to her kitchen. After sitting down at the bar, the Inspector pulled out a notebook and said, "Can you tell me how well you knew Sandy Stone?"

"Well, I only met him a few days ago on this cruise. But when I was pushed in Barbados, I found his business card on the ground. This helped me figure out that Sandy was a private investigator. But I couldn't figure out why he was on the ship."

"That's very interesting. I did not know that he was a PI. That could tie into his death if he learned something someone wasn't interested in finding out. Is there anything else that you can tell me?"

Iris took a moment to reply before saying, "Well, it seemed like he was getting close to Nora Brooks, the reporter. But nothing else comes to mind."

After closing his notebook, the Inspector said, "Thanks, you have been very helpful. I will take my leave now."

But before he left, Iris said, "Before you go, I wanted to ask. How do you think Sandy died?"

The Inspector looked surprised and said, "I'm not sure yet, but I'm suspecting poison. But I have to go now."

Iris innocently smiled as she replied, "Of course, Inspector." Then she watched him exit her cabin.

A short while later, Iris heard another knock on her door. Iris jumped up again, expecting it to be Nora this time. Once again, she headed to the door and opened it. Iris was glad to see Nora standing outside as Nora said, "Good afternoon, Iris. I was surprised to get your note. What is it you wanted to discuss with me?"

Iris felt a lump in her throat as she said, "Please come sit on the couch while I get you a drink."

Nora looked skeptical as she said, "Is everything all right? You seem worried about something. Does it have something to do with Sandy?"

Iris tried to speak, but before she got a chance, Nora saw the look on her face and started crying as she said, "No. Please don't tell me something bad happened to him."

Iris's voice trembled as she said, "I'm sorry to tell you this, but Sandy is no more," as she walked over to comfort Nora. A gut-wrenching wail escaped Nora's throat, and tears streamed down her face. Iris felt the raw pain of losing someone you cared about all over again as she embraced Nora, who sobbed uncontrollably.

A while later, Nora composed herself and said, "Sorry for letting you see that. I haven't cried that badly in a long time."

"No worries, dear. I am aware of how painful it can be to lose someone we care about."

"Thanks for understanding. I think I will go lie down for a little while."

"That sounds like a good idea, dear. But I'll be here for you if you need a friend later."

Nora gave a somber smile as she said, "Thanks, Iris. I appreciate it," before exiting the cabin and leaving Iris alone.

With a sense of urgency, Iris decided she couldn't wait any longer. She needed to search some of her suspect's rooms at dinner. So, she hastily made her way to the bathroom to take a shower, her mind already racing with the possibilities of what she might discover later during her search.

70

Present Day
Tuesday, August 12, 2024, 5:50 p.m.

It was finally dinner time, so Iris entered the hallway and got into position. She wanted to see if any of her suspects left for dinner before trying to search their cabins. So, she waited patiently for them to leave their cabins. A few minutes later, she saw Jordan and Selina leave their cabin and head toward the elevator. Good, she thought. Now, she needed to wait for her other suspects to leave their cabins. About ten minutes later, she spotted Georgia and Tyler exiting their rooms simultaneously and heading toward the elevator. It was good to note that both of their rooms were directly across the hall from each other. But just then, Iris remembered Nora had said she would lie down for a bit. That could throw a wrench into her plans if she entered the hallway later. But this was the best chance to do some sleuthing, so Iris took a chance. After waiting a few more minutes to be sure nobody else was going to show, Iris went quietly down the hall, pulled out the master key, unlocked the door, and entered Georgia's cabin.

Iris found it surprising that Georgia's cabin had the same layout as hers. But she was glad to see it since that should make searching easier. But since she wasn't sure what she was looking for, Iris just started walking around to see what stood out to her. As she walked through Georgia's bedroom, she noticed some shopping bags matching the brands of some of the Barbados stores. She wondered if she might find the disguise that was used when she got pushed in front of the taxi in Barbados. So, Iris searched the bags for a receipt or anything matching the disguise. But upon further inspection, Iris found neither. However, as she flipped through the bags, she found a bunch of clothes, a few fashion magazines, a copy of *Dial M for Murder*, a pair of diamond earrings, and a matching necklace. Nothing of interest, she thought, so she carefully returned the bags to their original place before continuing her search.

Iris ended up in Georgia's bathroom. Georgia had set up her bathroom to resemble a professional actor's dressing room, with various name-brand makeup products lining the sink. As she scanned the rest of the bathroom, she noticed some wall hooks next to the sink that held various colored wigs of professional quality. Seeing nothing else of interest, Iris went and checked the medicine cabinet. Inside, she saw a toothbrush, toothpaste, a bottle of facial cleanser, a jar of eye cream, a jar of moisturizer, a bottle of toner, a bottle of *Alprazolam*, a bottle of serum, a bottle of *Paracetamol*, some floss, and some teeth whitening strips. She couldn't believe how much stuff Georgia had crammed into this cabinet as she went to close it.

After she looked in the medicine cabinet, she went to see what was in the cabinet under the sink. It contained a hair dryer, some bath towels, and some lotion. Nothing of interest, Iris thought, as she went to close the sink cabinet. But as she was doing so, she noticed a glimpse of something shiny on the ground. So, after she closed the door, she bent down to see what it was. Upon closer inspection, she saw a small diamond earring, much like the pair she saw in Georgia's shopping bags. Iris reasoned that Georgia must have dropped this while doing makeup or changing clothes. So, after Iris finished examining it, she returned the earring to its original location to ensure that Georgia remained unaware of Iris's presence in her room. Afterward, Iris got up and exited the bathroom.

A few moments later, after finding nothing else of interest, Iris checked her phone for the time. The clock read 6:45 p.m. Dang, Iris thought. She probably wouldn't have much time to check out Tyler's cabin tonight. Oh well, Iris thought as she headed to Georgia's front door. Once there, she listened to the door to see if she heard any noise in the hallway. After a moment of silence, Iris opened the door gently and entered the hallway. After closing it, she went across the hall and entered Tyler's cabin.

Iris was glad that Tyler's cabin shared the same layout as hers. She didn't have much time, so she got to work. While scanning his bedroom, she noticed Tyler had a copy of *Gone Girl* on his nightstand. She also spotted a few shopping bags lying across his bed. So, she went and looked through them and found several new outfits and a bottle of rum from that rum shop that Iris had run into Tyler in Barbados. After she finished looking through the bags, she returned them to their proper place before moving on.

In the kitchen, Iris found some fashion magazines on the bar, a copy of the ship's itinerary, and a fruit bowl. Nothing of interest, she thought, so she went to check out the bathroom. The bathroom sink contained a toothbrush, a tube of toothpaste, a stick of deodorant, some lotion, and a bar of soap. Nothing of interest, so she looked in the medicine cabinet. Inside the cabinet was a bottle of ibuprofen, a bottle of eye drops, a bottle of *Tums*, *Q-tips*, some floss, a brow pen, a bottle of skin cleanser, a bottle of facial cleanser, a bottle of toner, a bottle of serum, a jar of eye cream, and a jar of moisturizer. Nothing caught her eye, so she closed it and looked under the sink.

Under the sink, Iris found extra bath towels, a hair dryer, a box of contacts, a bottle of eye solution, an extra bar of soap, shaving cream, a razor, and a bottle of aftershave. Nothing seemed important, so Iris closed it and checked the time on her phone. It read 7:05 p.m. She needed to leave before Tyler returned, so she headed to the front door. Once there, Iris checked to make sure she heard no noise. After calming her fears, she quickly opened the door and exited the cabin. Then she closed the door and headed towards the elevator to get her dinner. As she got there, the elevator opened, and Georgia and Tyler both exited simultaneously. Georgia seemed surprised to see her there as she said, "Good evening, sugar. Getting a late dinner tonight?"

Iris smiled as she tried to think of something. A moment later, she said, "Yeah, I took a nap earlier and overslept. So, I'm trying to get some food before they close."

Georgia laughed as Tyler said, "You got to get that beauty rest, girlfriend. I hope you have a nice dinner."

Iris smiled as she said, "Thanks. I'll try to." Then she watched the two move past her so she could enter the elevator. Once the doors closed, she sighed a breath of relief at how close she was to getting caught snooping. It was time for her reward. Iris thought as she rode the elevator to deck eight to get dinner.

71

Present Day
Tuesday, August 13, 2024, 8:15 p.m.

Upon entering the Italian restaurant, the hostess promptly seated Iris. Iris felt surprised to be seated quickly at a table, considering she arrived late for dinner. Not that she was complaining, and her stomach growled in response as if to prove a point. A moment later, a server appeared and took her order. While she waited for her food and drink to arrive, Iris planned her next move. Since another person had died, Iris thought she needed to look over the old case file again to see if she could find a connection to Sandy. She wanted to find Stacy Underwood's social media profiles and look for any potential clues there. That seemed like a good start, so Iris opened her internet browser and tried locating Stacy's old accounts.

After clicking several links, Iris finally found an old *Instagram* account for Stacy Underwood. As she scrolled through the feed, Iris noticed an odd number of scuba diving photos with Stacy's sister, Mary, tagged in them as well. It was an odd coincidence that Stacy and Nora also liked scuba diving. Iris wondered if that was the missing link as she continued to scroll. Further down, she found several pictures of them on beaches and other types of nature preserves. That went back for months. But no pictures of her with Charles. How strange, she thought as she closed the app. A moment later, her food arrived, and Iris focused on the task at hand.

After dinner, Iris headed to the library to continue her research. After sitting at the computer, Iris opened the internet browser and continued her research. She started by logging into her email and looking at the old case files her son had sent her to see if she had overlooked something. As she scanned through the files, the words *Long Legs* popped up, and Iris had a revelation. The files discussed Charles being seen outside the strip club shortly after Stacy disappeared. That also was the place Georgia used to work for before she got hired to work at *Southern Belles*. She wasn't sure if the club was still open. So, Iris opened a new tab and looked it up. A moment later, the business popped up with an address and working hours. Perfect, she thought as she took a picture of the information. She would have to get her son to question the workers there to see if anyone recognized seeing Georgia and Charles together at the club. Switching back over to the files, she scanned some more.

A short while later, she realized there was no new information to find, so she closed the email and switched back to *Google*. She searched her suspect's social media to see if she had overlooked anything. However, as she slowly went through the pages, she thought she had hit a dead end until she finally found something new on Tyler's *Instagram*. A picture popped up from the spring before Stacy disappeared featuring Tyler at a beach with his arm wrapped around the shoulder of a handsome young man. This photo caught Iris's attention because the man tagged in the photo was named Ryan Sterling. Shock came across her face at the realization that Tyler had dated her son's newest boyfriend almost ten years ago. It was an odd coincidence, but she couldn't see what it could do with the murder. But other than that, she couldn't find anyone else of interest. Now, it was time for her to return to her cabin, call her son, and update him on her findings.

Back in her room, Iris started a fresh pot of coffee before calling her son since she knew she would have to stay up late tonight to search Sandy's room undetected. After getting the coffee, she sat on the couch and called her son. A few moments later, he answered and said, "Good evening, Mom. I hope to hear that you've been staying out of trouble."

Iris laughed awkwardly as she said, "I haven't gotten into any trouble."

"Glad to hear that. I was half worried you had gotten yourself into a mess."

Once again, Iris awkwardly laughed as she said, "Well, I didn't really get into a mess, but I found Sandy dead earlier today. The inspector suspects that someone might have poisoned him."

Samuel groaned as he said, "That's horrible. It seems like you keep getting dragged into this case. What happened exactly?"

Iris went into detail about what had happened. After she finished, she said, "I know you don't want me involved, but Sandy's death has to be connected to Charles somehow. And I know that someone hired Sandy. Most likely, Charles. And I think Sandy found someone and got killed for it."

"That's a reasonable guess. But it's not your job to investigate. That's the job of the inspector, Mom."

"I know, son, but I don't think the Inspector is doing an excellent job so far. I found some leads that might help solve this, but I need your help to check them out."

"I'm not saying I'm going to help, but what are these leads you found?"

"Well, I got a few things I wanted you to check out. First, I learned Georgia worked as a dancer at a club called *Long Legs*. I want you to go there and ask to see if anyone remembers seeing her with Charles ten years ago. Second, I want you to look into the car accidents of Jordan's parents and see if there was any shady business going on, and then I want you to see how close it relates to Inga Lagman's death. The third thing I want you to do is go to Sandy's business and check it out for clues. Maybe see if you can figure out what led him on the cruise. And the last thing isn't probably relevant, but I also learned that Tyler used to date your boyfriend, Ryan. I wondered if you could ask Ryan about their breakup and if he knew how Tyler and Georgia met."

Samuel sighed as he said, "That's quite a list of things to do. And I'm not sure about the last one. We just started dating, and it might be awkward."

"I know it's a lot to ask, but tomorrow is Wednesday, and time is running out. If we don't catch the killer by Friday, they might escape justice. And as for Ryan, he knows you're a cop, so say it's for a case. It's not as if you're lying or being dishonest."

"I guess, but I'm unsure how quickly I can complete all this. I can try to get your answers back by tomorrow night, but I cannot make any promises."

"Thanks, Sammy. You're the best. But I'll let you go now."

"Yeah, whatever you say," Samuel laughed as he continued, "Goodnight, Mom," before hanging up.

Iris sat down on her bed and turned on the TV to kill time until she could set her plan of searching Sandy's room into action.

72

Present Day
Wednesday, August 14, 2024, 12:15 a.m.

It was finally time for Iris to search Sandy's room. She felt shivers go down her spine as she quietly opened her door and entered the hallway. She slowly tiptoed down the hall until she got to Sandy's door. Thankfully, there wasn't any crime scene tape put up. So, Iris withdrew the master key from her purse and opened the door. After entering, she quickly but quietly shut it. Then she turned on the flashlight on her phone and got to work.

As Iris delved deeper into Sandy's room, she stumbled upon his wallet. Inside, she discovered his driver's license and a private investigator license, confirming his profession. The wallet also held a substantial amount of cash, a detail that didn't surprise Iris. She returned the wallet to its place and proceeded to the kitchen, her mind buzzing with questions.

On the bar, Iris found a manila folder and a notebook. She flipped through the folder and saw news articles containing photographs of Stacy Underwood. Iris had forgotten how beautiful Stacy was. She wondered what happened the day Stacy disappeared as she flipped through the folder. As she reached the end, Iris saw a contract. As she read it, she realized it was a contract between Sandy and Charles. Charles had hired Sandy to investigate a potential connection between Nora and Stacy. It seemed like Charles thought Nora had some information regarding Stacy's current whereabouts. At the end of the document, Iris spotted Sandy and Charles's signature. She was impressed by Charles's neat signature instead of Sandy's chicken scratch as she returned the papers to the folder and placed them back on the bar. Then she picked up the notebook and flipped through it. Sandy had written notes about the case inside the notebook. The last entry she found was a circled statement he had written saying, Nora and Stacy related? Guilty of murder? How interesting, Iris thought. It made her wonder why Sandy thought Nora and Stacy were related. Maybe it had something to do with the fact they were both reporters and had enjoyed scuba diving in their free time. Iris wished she knew how they knew each other. But just then, a memory resurfaced of Nora talking on the phone with someone and saying I love you too. This made Iris wonder if Nora was talking to Stacy. She would have to ask Nora tomorrow morning to see how she would react. But for now, she needed to look for more clues, so she returned to her search.

Iris went to check out Sandy's bathroom for clues. On the bathroom sink, she spotted a toothbrush, a tube of toothpaste, and a bar of soap. Nothing of interest, so she checked the medicine cabinet. Inside, she found a stick of deodorant, a box of *Q-tips*, some floss, a bottle of mouthwash, and a bottle of *Tums*. Nothing stood out, so Iris closed it and checked under the sink. All she found was some extra towels and a hairdryer. This was a bust, Iris thought as she closed the door to the sink. Iris concluded that she had found all the clues she could find in Sandy's cabin, so she left the bathroom and returned to her cabin for the night.

73

Present Day
Wednesday, August 14, 2024, 9:00 a.m.

Iris sat in the top row of the movie theater with popcorn in her lap and a drink by her side. As the lights dimmed, the giant movie screen came to life. But the odd thing was that instead of a movie, the screen showed Charles Underwood pushing his wife off their yacht. Iris watched in shock as he went and caused the yacht to tip. Then the scene jumped to Charles leaving the *Long Legs* club by the back entrance. But he didn't see the undercover reporter take a picture of him with a Polaroid camera in the distance as he got in his car and drove away. Then, a moment later, Iris heard a loud blast as she opened her eyes. After realizing it was her alarm, Iris turned it off as she got her bearings. How strange, she thought as she stretched and got out of bed. As Iris gathered fresh clothes for the day, she wondered what her strange dream was about. It seemed odd to her because certain facts didn't line up with her dream. But as she headed to the shower, Iris mused that most dreams differed vastly from real life.

After taking her shower, Iris went to the kitchen and started a pot of coffee. While waiting, she tried to review her to-do list for the day. She needed to question her various suspects about different things. But first, she wanted to talk to Nora. If she was lucky, she might locate her in her room. So, she needed to head there first. Besides that, Iris remembered she had an appointment at the spa and salon that day. She might run into some of her suspects there if she was lucky. Otherwise, she would have to track them down. Iris felt like she was getting close to solving this case. But she felt there was a crucial clue she was missing. Hopefully, her son will locate that information today. Otherwise, she was running out of time. She only had today and tomorrow to figure out what happened before the killer escaped justice, and her husband's cold case would remain unsolved. So, she had to get things wrapped up. That sounded like a plan. Iris smiled as she went to check on her coffee. It was done, so she went and poured herself a cup and sat down at the bar. After finishing her coffee, Iris got up and put the cup in the sink before grabbing her purse and heading off to Nora's cabin.

Iris walked up to Nora's cabin door and knocked. After a few moments, the door opened, and Iris saw Nora dressed in a nightgown, still half asleep. Nora yawned loudly before saying, "Morning, Iris. Is there something I can help you with?"

Iris smiled as she said, "Good morning, Nora. I came to see you because I had something important to discuss with you. But I think it would be better if we didn't discuss it in the hall. So may I please come inside?"

Nora looked intrigued as she said, "Sure thing. I'm curious to hear what you have to say," before opening the door and letting Iris inside.

Once inside, Nora led Iris to the kitchen bar and motioned for her to sit. But as she did so, Iris noticed a couple of sketchbooks lying on the bar, with a couple of pencils and a cup of coffee beside them. After sitting down, Nora asked, "Would you like some coffee before we start?"

"Sure, I wouldn't mind a cup. Black is fine for me."

So, Nora poured a cup of coffee and brought it to Iris. After Iris took the cup, Nora sat across from her and asked, "So, what do you want to discuss?"

"I wanted to ask what your connection to Stacy Underwood is."

Nora turned pale as she said, "What do you mean? There is no connection. I didn't even know her."

"I don't believe you. I found out that you both worked as reporters and knew how to scuba dive. Not to mention the fact that Charles hired Sandy to investigate a connection between you and Stacy."

"Those are all coincidences. We might have worked in the same job field, but we worked for different companies, and I didn't start scuba diving until after Stacy had disappeared, so that proves nothing. As for Charles hiring Sandy to look for a connection, this is the first I ever heard of it. I do not know why he thought I knew anything about his wife."

Iris was trying to think of a rebuff. She knew something was there but couldn't figure out what she was missing. But just then, an idea struck her, and she said, "How old are you?"

Nora looked surprised as she said, "I'm fifty. Why are you asking?"

Bingo thought Iris as she felt the various pieces fall into place as she said, "You're Stacy Underwood, aren't you?"

Nora appeared physically ill as she asked, "How did you figure it out?"

"Well, it's the only thing that makes sense regarding Charles wanting to hire Sandy to shadow you. Plus, you work the same job, scuba dive, and are the same age. Those are a lot of coincidences to consider."

Nora sighed as she said, "Fair enough, I suppose. But don't think I killed Charles or Sandy just because I'm Charles's missing wife. I was completely surprised to learn that he was on the same cruise I won a trip on this week."

Iris felt happy having solved her late husband's cold case

regarding what happened to Stacy, but she still had unanswered questions. One was all of her suspects having claimed to win a trip onboard the cruise. She wondered who had paid for these tickets. Charles perhaps. But if he had known Nora was Stacy, then why hire Sandy? Unless he wasn't sure. And why bring everyone else? Something didn't add up. And was Nora telling the truth? Iris wasn't sure. Even though it seemed like Nora had the best motive for the murders, Iris believed Nora when she said she didn't do it. But where did that leave her? Maybe Nora could clear up some past questions concerning her disappearance and Inga's death and help untangle this mess. So, Iris said, "Tell me more about your disappearance and Inga's death. I want to understand the connection between the past and the present case."

Nora sighed as she said, "Long story short, my sister Mary and I planned my escape. We practiced scuba diving, so when I faked my death, I could swim to safety and wouldn't have to worry about Charles trying to locate me. He was abusive, a cheater, and a thief, to name a few, and I didn't want to live that lifestyle anymore, so I escaped and started my new life as Nora. As for Inga, I'm not sure if Charles killed her for discovering he was stealing from his company or for his cheating. However, I am certain that he was involved, even if he did not commit the murder himself."

"I know it doesn't help, but I'm sorry that Charles hurt you in the past. And I can understand why you faked your death to escape. Nobody should have to experience that or live that way. But I can't let Charles or Sandy's murder go unsolved. Despite Charles being a horrible, vile person, he didn't deserve to be murdered. And justice needs to be served. Do you think that your disappearance or Inga's death is linked to the deaths of Charles and Sandy?"

Nora took a moment before saying, "I don't see how my disappearance would be linked to their deaths. So, maybe it has something to do with Inga's death. But I don't see how that is possible since that was almost ten years ago."

"That is the issue. If there was no connection to your

disappearance, then maybe someone sought revenge for Inga's death. But that was such a long time ago unless, maybe, the tenth anniversary brought up old feelings, and someone finally bubbled over like a volcano, like her daughter, Selina. Do you know anything about Inga's daughter Selina or Jordan, your husband's, intern that summer? I'm asking because they are both on the cruise and are engaged. You might have seen them at trivia or karaoke night, too."

Nora looked shocked and said, "No, I wasn't aware they were on board or were a couple. As for back then, I don't recall having met either of them. Although there is something fuzzy in the back of my mind, I can't recall it now."

"That's unfortunate," began Iris before continuing, "Hopefully, you'll remember what it was later. As for now, I think you need to talk to the Inspector and tell him who you are and what your side of things is before he finds out and tries to arrest you."

Nora sighed as she replied, "You're right. I'll call him in a minute. But I would prefer to do it alone if possible."

Iris smiled as she said, "Sure thing. I'll leave you to it then," before getting up, leaving, and heading to breakfast.

74

Present Day
Wednesday, August 14, 2024, 10:00 a.m.

Iris entered the cafe and smelled freshly baked pastries and freshly ground coffee beans as she approached the counter. After ordering and paying for a blueberry muffin, Iris looked around while she waited for her muffin. Unfortunately, she didn't spot any of her suspects. A moment later, her order was ready. Iris retrieved her muffin and headed to a table.

As she ate her muffin, Iris wondered where she should head next. She had some time to kill before her spa and salon appointment in the early afternoon. Maybe a dip in the pool, or she could hit the gym for a bit. As Iris considered the possibilities, her gaze caught Georgia standing in line at the counter. What luck, thought Iris as she watched Georgia in line. Iris reasoned she should try to question Georgia after she received her order. A few moments later, she got her chance. Georgia received her order and headed to a table. Iris waited a few moments before getting up from her table, approaching

Georgia, and saying, "Good morning, Georgia. How are you doing?"

Georgia looked up surprisingly and skeptically as she said, "Good morning, sweetheart. I'm doing all right. I just got myself some breakfast this morning."

Iris noticed that Tyler wasn't around and said, "I can't help but notice that your friend Tyler isn't here this morning. Is he doing all right?"

"Funny you should mention that sugar. He wasn't feeling well this morning. I think he may have had too much to drink last night."

"Oh dear," began Iris before continuing, "That doesn't sound good. Hopefully, he feels better."

"I hope so, too. But what is your true purpose for being here, Iris?"

Iris's cheeks flushed as she mustered the courage to ask, "I couldn't help but wonder, where did you and Tyler first cross paths?"

Georgia looked surprised as she said, "Well, we met about ten years ago. Back when I worked as a dancer at a club. He used to do my makeup. Why are you asking?"

"Well, would that club happen to be *Long Legs*?"

Georgia's face contorted with frustration as she retorted, "I won't confirm or deny that. If you'll excuse me, I'd like to enjoy my breakfast in peace."

Iris smiled as she said, "Sure thing. Sorry to have bothered you," before returning to her table. That certainly upset her, mused Iris as she finished her muffin. Afterward, she got up, left the cafe, and returned to her room.

75

Present Day
Wednesday, August 14, 2024, 10:30 a.m.

*A*s Iris strolled down the hallway to her room, she noticed Jordan and Selina exiting their cabin, dressed in swimsuits. This sparked an idea in her mind. She continued towards her cabin, biding her time. After a few minutes, she glanced down the hallway, ensuring no one was in sight. Satisfied, she made her move. Iris returned to Jordan and Selina's cabin, master key in hand, and unlocked the door. Stepping inside, she shut the door swiftly, her heart pounding with anticipation.

Like before, the layout was the same as the other cabins. As Iris looked around, she noticed some magazines on the coffee table. She thumbed through them and spotted a copy of *Cosmopolitan*, *National Geographic*, *People Magazine*, and *Travel and Leisure*. Nothing of interest, or so it seemed. On the bar sat two coffee cups, perhaps a clue to their morning routine. In the sink, Iris spotted a silver platter, a potential sign of a recent meal. As she went to the bedroom, she guessed the couple had ordered room service this morning, a detail that could be significant in the investigation.

In the bedroom, Iris spotted a copy of *Evil Under the Sun* on the nightstand. On the one opposite of it sat a copy of *The Woman in Cabin 10*. She also spotted a few shopping bags on the floor. She flipped through them and found a couple of blouses, skirts, earrings, nail polish, T-shirts, shorts, flip-flops, and a bathing suit. After placing the bags back on the floor, Iris headed to the bathroom.

The bathroom looked messy, with the sink covered with lower-end makeup products, a bottle of lotion, some skin care products, a hairdryer, and a brush. A soap bar was also in a dish next to two electric toothbrushes. Opening the medicine cabinet, Iris spotted some dental floss, a bottle of mouthwash, some deodorant, a bottle of *Tums*, some *Tylenol*, a bottle of *Escitalopram*, some *Q-tips*, some shaving cream, some razors, a bottle of *Dextroamphetamine*, and some band-aids.

After closing the cabinet, Iris looked under the sink but only found some bath towels. Satisfied that nothing else was interesting, Iris returned to the front door. After pressing an ear to the door, she listened for any noise but heard nothing, so Iris opened the door, exited, shut the door, and returned to her room.

After changing into her swimsuit, Iris grabbed her book off the nightstand and put it in her purse before exiting her cabin. Then she made her way to the pool. Once there, she looked around, trying to locate Jordan or Selina. After a few moments, she located them sitting by the poolside, approached them, and said, "Good morning, guys. How are you doing?"

The couple looked at Iris before Selina said, "Oh, good morning, Iris. We were dipping our feet in the pool. How are you doing?"

"I'm doing all right. I wondered if the inspector had questioned you about Sandy's death yet?"

The couple looked concerned as Jordan said, "Yes, he came by and talked to us last night. But unfortunately, we had nothing to tell him. We had never met the man before this cruise. It's a very sad business, though."

"It is very sad. A young life has been lost, and I plan on solving his murder. I discovered he was a private investigator hired by Charles to shadow someone on this cruise. Do you have any idea who that could be?"

Once again, the couple looked concerned. They sat silently as they looked at each other before Selina said, "We do not know. As Jordan said, we have never met the man before."

"True, but you both knew Charles and had issues with him. You accused him of having murdered your mom, and Jordan also worked with your mom and was dating you at the same time as well. Not to mention, you both held a grudge against him. Maybe Charles hired Sandy to get dirt on you so you wouldn't try to get revenge on him."

"That's preposterous," Jordan exclaimed, his voice rising before he quickly lowered it, "We would never do such a thing. Besides, that was a decade ago. Why would we wait until now to act?"

"Well, Charles is a man of wealth. Maybe you saw him on board the ship and took a chance. Maybe the tenth anniversary of Inga's death brought up past feelings that bubbled over."

Selina looked angry as tears fell down her face as she said, "You're crazy. We did no such thing. I might have wanted to kill Charles years ago, but I've learned to release my hate because it only holds you back from happiness."

"I'm sorry..." began Iris, but she got cut off by Jordan, who said, "Please leave. You already caused us enough trouble on this trip. If you want to find Charles and Sandy's killer, look elsewhere."

Iris nodded as she got up and left, a mix of guilt and determination weighing on her. She couldn't help but notice Jordan hugging Selina and comforting her, a sight that tugged at her heart. But she knew she had to cover her bases, to follow every lead. She knew Charles had hired Sandy to check into Nora's background, but she wanted to see how the couple reacted. She couldn't cross them off her suspect list until she heard what Samuel said tonight. For now, they both still had a motive. But for now, she needed to relax until it was time for her spa and salon appointment. So, she found a lounge chair, laid down, opened her book, and read, her mind still racing with the mysteries of the cruise. But a short while later, the ship's intercom came on and said, "Good morning, everyone. This is your captain speaking. I have an important announcement to make. Due to some unfortunate circumstances, the S.S. Paradise must dock back in St. Lucia temporarily. I'm sorry for any inconvenience this may cause you. We hope to get the situation resolved as soon as possible. If you have any questions, please call the help desk from your cabin, and they will do their best to accommodate you. Otherwise, I hope you all have a wonderful day aboard the SS Paradise."

Iris wondered what that was about. She wondered if that vaguely referred to both deaths on the cruise or if something else was going on. She guessed she should call that help desk later and ask some questions. But she was sure it was busy, full of confused and angry people wondering how late this recent development would set their cruise back. Iris wondered herself but knew she wouldn't get the answers right now. So, she returned to her book and waited for the phone lines to die down.

76

Present Day
Wednesday, August 14, 2024, 1:30 p.m.

Iris closed her book with a satisfied smile on her face. She guessed the killer in her book correctly. If only it were that easy in real life, mused Iris. The mystery she was currently entangled in felt like a puzzle with missing pieces. She felt like she was close to figuring out who the killer was. But she still needed a few things cleared up before being sure. Hopefully, she will have a clearer answer tonight after talking to her son after dinner. But Iris needed to check the time to see how much she had before her salon and spa appointment. So, she pulled out her phone and saw that the time was 1:30 p.m. She still had a little bit of time before her appointment. Maybe now would be a good time to get lunch and maybe call that help desk for some answers. Just then, her stomach growled as if giving a response. Iris laughed and thought, message received, as she got up from her lounge chair and gathered her things before returning to her room.

Once inside, Iris sat down with her things in her room before changing her clothes. Then she called room service and ordered an egg salad sandwich and a glass of sweet tea. Afterward, she went to her bedroom and called the help desk. A quick inquiry told her the reason the ship was turning around was more or less what the captain had said on the intercom. So, that was a dead end—not that Iris was surprised. She sighed as she turned on the TV and watched part of *Death on the Nile* while waiting for lunch.

A short while later, Iris heard a knock on the door. She paused her movie as she got up and answered the door. After paying for her food, Iris returned to her bedroom and hit the play button on her remote as she removed the lid on her platter and ate her lunch.

After eating, Iris checked the time. It was 2:45 p.m. She had to get ready for her appointment, so she placed her platter in the sink before grabbing her purse and heading out.

Iris lay face down on the massage table, listening to the soothing sounds of water falling in the background as her massage therapist performed her geriatric massage. The scent of lavender filled the air, adding to the relaxing atmosphere. Iris felt like she was in heaven as the therapist worked her magic, applying gentle strokes to her back. The sound of the music brought a tranquil feeling over Iris, and she closed her eyes and let the stress of the cruise wash away. A while later, Iris was awakened by the sound of the massage therapist saying, "Excuse me, Miss, but your massage is finished."

Iris blushed as she rose from the table and said, "I'm so sorry. The sound of the music and your gentle touch must have put me to sleep."

The therapist reassured Iris by saying, "No worries, Miss. This happens a lot. I'm glad you enjoyed yourself."

Iris reassured the woman before getting up and exiting the spa. Then she headed over next door to the salon.

At the salon, a staff member led Iris to a styling chair and seated her. While she waited for her hairstylist to appear, Iris scanned the salon, hoping to spot Tyler, with no success. A few moments later, her hairstylist appeared and got to work.

A while later, the hairstylist finished washing and styling Iris's hair and said, "Tada, darling. Please get up and see what you think at one of the giant dressing mirrors."

Iris got up and complied with the hairstylist's suggestion. Looking into the giant dressing mirror surrounded by lights, she smiled at the image that stood back at her. The hairstylist had styled her shiny gray hair in a way that was both elegant and modern, a short, messy cut with side bangs, which framed her face in a complimentary way and brought attention to her blue eyes. Iris turned and smiled at the hairstylist, saying, "It looks wonderful. I love it!"

The hairstylist smiled as he said, "Fabulous, darling. I hope you have a wonderful day on the SS Paradise," before motioning her to exit the salon.

As Iris headed towards the exit, she spotted Tyler sitting in the waiting area reading a fashion magazine. How fortunate, she thought as she approached Tyler and said, "Good afternoon, Tyler. How are you doing, dear?"

Tyler looked from his celebrity gossip magazine in surprise as he said, "Oh, good afternoon, girlfriend. I'm doing all right. I'm just waiting for my appointment. But from the look of things, you just got your hair done. It looks fabulous, girl!"

Iris blushed as she said, "Oh, thanks, dear. I appreciate it. Sorry to bother you, but I just wanted to ask if the inspector has come and questioned you about poor Sandy's death yet?"

Tyler's eyes widened with surprise as he replied, "As a matter of fact, he did last night. However, I had little to tell him except that I saw Sandy hanging out with that older woman, Nora, a few times during the cruise. Do you think that's why the ship is turning back around?"

"I'm not sure, but it makes sense considering what also happened to Charles Underwood. The captain probably didn't want to scare everyone onboard and cause a panic."

"You might be right, but that's a job for the police if that's the case. I'm just here to relax and stay out of people's business. Hopefully, whatever the reason is, it gets resolved soon so we can head back to Orlando."

Before Iris could reply, a receptionist called out Tyler's name. He said, "Sorry, but I have to go," before he set the magazine down and left. But as he did so, Iris glimpsed the cover. It was a copy of *Star* magazine with an image of Harry Styles and a caption below it that read, *Pop Star Considering Retirement?!* Read more to hear all the juicy details facing his future musical career. The image gave Iris an idea as she headed back to her room.

77

Present Day
Wednesday, August 14, 2024, 8: 30 a.m.

Samuel unlocked his car, got inside, and started it before heading to work. A few moments later, he pulled his phone out of his pocket and called his boyfriend, Ryan. Two rings later, Samuel heard Ryan say, "Good morning, handsome. How are you doing?"

Samuel smiled, saying, "I'm doing all right, babe. But I have a question for you. What can you tell me about your ex, Tyler Reed, and how your relationship with him was like ten years ago? It's related to a case I'm working on. Also, do you remember him hanging out with a woman named Georgia Fisher back then?"

Ryan laughed, saying, "Wow, I didn't expect to hear that name again. That brings back some memories. But there isn't much to tell. We dated back in high school, and I broke up with him after I graduated. I wanted to explore college without being in a relationship, and Tyler was still in high school. He didn't take it well, but it was our first romantic relationship, so that's understandable. As for Georgia, she was his best friend back then. They were always hanging out and doing stuff together. But I felt like she was a bad influence on him, being a stripper. She even helped him get a job at the club where she worked as a makeup artist. But that was years ago. I don't even know if they're still friends or what jobs they have now. Does any of that help?"

Samuel wasn't sure. It didn't seem like much new information had been discovered. But at least he checked the lead out. Maybe he would have better luck with the car wreck reports at work. So, he said, "I'm not sure. But I appreciate your input. I'll explain more later when we have dinner tonight. Until then, have a good day, babe."

Samuel waited until he heard Ryan say in an endearing tone, "Ok, handsome. Talk to you later, bye," before hanging up. A few moments later, he arrived at work.

A LITTLE WHILE LATER, SAMUEL HAD A BREAK FROM HIS work, so he pulled up the website on his computer to look up the car accident reports. Once the website loaded, he typed in the necessary information to look up Inga Lagman's records. After hitting the enter key, the report loaded on the screen. After scanning the document, Samuel discovered that Inga Lagman's car accident was still classified as an unsolved hit-and-run. So, unfortunately, there was no new information. So, he switched over to look up Jordan's parent's car accident. When the report showed up, Samuel quickly scanned through the information. He saw it mentioned that the car had faulty brake pads that failed to work during a severe thunderstorm. How interesting, he thought. It made Samuel wonder if someone might have tampered with the brakes. The only issue was that since it happened so long ago, there was no way to research it further, which frustrated him. A few moments later, Samuel's phone alarm interrupted his thoughts, signaling that it was time for his lunch break. After turning off his alarm, he quickly closed the tabs and logged out of his computer before he got up from his desk and headed to his car.

As Samuel pulled into the parking lot, he searched for Sandy's business. But didn't see it. So, he drove slowly down the strip mall, hoping to spot it. After a few moments, he found it in the far-right-hand corner of the strip mall. After parking, he turned off his car and walked up to the business.

As he looked around, he spotted some discreet security cameras facing the door of the business. When he reached the front door, he noticed a note on it that said the business was temporarily closed until 8/16. He also spotted Sandy's work hours, which read that appointments could be made on the *Eye Spy* website. Walk-ins are not guaranteed. Samuel thought that limited his access as he headed back to his car. Once inside, he opened his lunch bag and ate before returning to work.

SAMUEL JUST ARRIVED OUTSIDE THE CLUB GEORGIA USED TO work at, *Long Legs*. He was surprised at how run-down the place looked, making him wonder if it was still in business. A moment later, Samuel got an answer when an older woman came out of the front entrance smoking a cigarette. From the look of things, Samuel assumed that the woman was a dancer. Maybe this was his lucky break. So, he got out of his car and approached the woman.

The woman spoke in a rough voice that came from years of smoking, "Sorry honey, we don't open for another hour. I'm just out here on my smoke break."

Samuel smiled politely before replying, "That's fine. I'm here to ask some questions for a case." He pulled his police badge out of his wallet and showed it to the woman.

This caused the woman to jump at the sight of it, dropping her cigarette. A moment later, the woman let out a curse word under her breath at the sight before regaining her composure and saying, "Oh, I didn't realize you were a cop. What questions do you have, handsome?"

Samuel pulled out his phone, pulled up an old photo of Georgia, and showed it to the woman before saying, "I wanted to know if you recognized this woman. She used to work here about ten years ago."

The woman looked like she had seen a ghost as she gasped, "That's Peaches. Did something happen to her?"

"No worries. She is alive and in good health. My questions concern a man she might have known back in the day. His name is Charles Underwood. Does that name ring any bells?"

"Yes, it does. He came in a lot about ten years ago and started courting Peaches. He even got her pregnant before he left her and broke her heart. And to add insult to injury, she even lost the baby in the end. It was a very sad business for her. Soon after, she got recruited and began her career in modeling. I'm glad to hear that she's doing well now. Does that answer your question?"

"Yes, it does. Thank you so much for your help!"

"No problem, handsome. My name is Chardonnay if you decide to come and see me again during working hours."

"Sorry, but I can't. I'm gay, plus I have a boyfriend."

Chardonnay laughed before pulling a pack of cigarettes out of her purse. Then she took one out of the pack and lit it before taking a long puff and saying, "Dang, all the cute guys are married or gay. Well, it was nice to meet you, handsome. I got to head back in a moment for rehearsal."

Samuel nodded in understanding before saying, "No worries. I was about to head out, anyway. Take care, Chardonnay."

Chardonnay took another hit off her cigarette before stubbing it out and saying, "Thanks, you too," before heading back inside the building. So, Samuel returned to his car and headed home.

78

Present Day
Wednesday, August 14, 2024, 5:30 p.m.

As Iris walked down the hallway to her room, she felt the urge to check on Nora as she passed her cabin but decided not to at the last moment. Iris wondered if Nora had talked to the Inspector yet as she reached her cabin.

Once inside, she got ready for dinner. But since she had just been to the spa and salon, there wasn't much to do before she left again. As she passed Nora's cabin, she knocked on the door this time. After a moment of silence, she tried knocking again, then said, "Nora, it's Iris. I just wanted to see how you're doing."

Again, there was more silence. Iris worried a little but shrugged it off, reasoning that Nora must have left for dinner already. She turned and headed down the hall to the elevator. As she got in and pressed the button, Iris hoped she would see Nora again soon.

As she entered the Mexican restaurant, the host greeted Iris and led her to her table. After being seated, Iris looked around, hoping to spot Nora, to no avail. Iris felt uneasy but reasoned that she was just being paranoid.

After dinner, Iris headed back to her floor. She was eager to catch Nora and put her fears to rest. Exiting the elevator, she practically ran down the hall until she stood outside Nora's cabin. She felt nervous as she slowly raised her hand to knock on the door. Like earlier, there was no response. Something felt off. Iris raised her voice, saying, "Nora, if you're in there, please answer. Otherwise, I'm going to come inside."

After a few minutes of silence, Iris withdrew the master key from her purse and said, "Okay, I'm coming in, Nora," before unlocking and opening the door.

As she stepped inside, she went to the bar and screamed as she saw Nora lying face down at the bar. As she went to feel her pulse, she saw lying next to Nora on the counter an empty bottle of vodka, her empty prescription bottle of *Xanax*, a coffee cup, and a handwritten suicide note. After determining that Nora was dead, Iris cried. After regaining her composure, Iris looked at the note and read it.

To whom it may concern,

If you are reading this, I'm here to confess to the murders of Charles Underwood and Sandy Stone. My true identity is Stacy Underwood, and I feared my husband, Charles, would find out who I was and seek revenge on me all these years later. I later discovered that Charles had hired Sandy to investigate Nora's connection to Stacy Underwood. I worried he would figure out who I was, so I killed my husband and Sandy to protect my new identity. I feel guilty for what I've done, so I've decided to end my life. I'm sorry for those I've hurt, and I hope you can forgive me.

Sincerely,

Stacy Underwood

Iris was in shock at what she had just seen. She couldn't believe that Nora / Stacy had committed suicide. If only Iris had gone to the Inspector earlier, she might have prevented this from happening. But what ifs wouldn't change the fact that Nora was dead, yet something about the entire scene felt off, but Iris couldn't tell what. Maybe it would come to her after the shock wore off. But for now, she needed to call the captain and report what she found out. So, she pulled out her phone and called the captain. After a few rings, he answered, and Iris explained what had happened. After she finished, the captain replied, "I'll tell the Inspector, and he will be there as soon as possible. Please don't touch anything." Iris assured him she wouldn't before hanging up.

A short while later, Inspector Arabz arrived and asked, "Please tell me how you found the body."

"Well, I talked to Nora this morning and figured out that she was Stacy Underwood. She admitted the fact and explained what had happened. Then I told her to talk to you and explain her story. She said she would. But I wanted to see if she had, so before dinner, I checked on her to see what happened but got no response. So, I tried again after dinner. After not hearing anything again, I opened the door using the master key I borrowed from the captain to come in and check on her, and that's when I found her."

The Inspector looked at Iris suspiciously before saying, "I need you to return the master key you borrowed from the captain."

Iris blushed as she handed over the key to the Inspector. After putting it in his pocket, he asked, "Did Nora act strange before you left her cabin this morning?"

Iris tried to reflect on this morning before saying, "No, I don't think so. She seemed like she was going to talk to you soon after. But Nora acted like she knew she should talk to you but wasn't thrilled to do so."

"That makes sense. But did she not act or speak like she was considering suicide?"

"Not at all. I'm still not convinced it is suicide. She said nothing about being involved in the murders. She acted surprised that she had won a trip on the same cruise as Charles. And she's not the first to mention having won a trip on the cruise. So, I think there is something more going on here. I have a theory, but I am not completely sure yet."

"Who told you they had won a trip this week?"

"Nora Brooks, Sandy Stone, Selina Lagman, Jordan

Mateo, Georgia Fisher, and Tyler Reed all told me they won a trip on this cruise."

"I'll have to question all of them again. But so far, Nora seems to have the best motive. Do you have a theory that could change my mind?"

"Well, I have an idea, but I'm unsure how to connect it to Nora's death. There's something off about the crime scene, but I can't figure out what it is."

"Well, Charles and Sandy were both killed with a mix of alcohol and *Xanax*, and Nora had her empty prescription bottle next to her. If she didn't do it, how can you explain that?"

A thought came to Iris as she said, "Did the autopsy reveal what type of *Xanax* was used in the murders?"

"No, just the amount in the system. Why are you asking?"

"I was just curious. Do you know if these murders are why the ship is returning to St. Lucia?"

"I'm not at liberty to say. But I think you can figure it out if you got this far with your poking and prodding."

Iris blushed as she said, "Fair enough. Can I go now, Inspector?"

The Inspector looked intrigued and said, "Sure, you're free to go, but I might have more questions later."

Iris nodded in understanding before taking off to her room.

79

Present Day
Wednesday, August 14, 2024, 8:00 p.m.

Iris sat down on the couch. After getting comfortable, she pulled out her phone and called her son. After a few rings, she heard him say, "Good evening, Mom. I got your research done. Here is what I found out…"

After he finished his report, Iris said, "Thanks for the information, Sammy. I think it will be very helpful in my investigation. But we have an additional problem. This morning, I went and talked to Nora and figured out she was Stacy Underwood, living a new life under a new name. But I found her dead after dinner from an apparent suicide with a note confessing to the murders. However, I think she was murdered, but I cannot prove it."

"That's crazy, Mom. That had to be tough to find. I'm sorry you had to see that. Can you tell me what the crime scene looked like? Maybe I can help you figure out a clue to prove that it was murder."

"All right, dear. This is what I saw…"

A few moments later, Samuel said, "I think I figured it

out. Why would she put vodka in her coffee and then mix it with her *Xanax* when the other two murders happened with just alcohol and *Xanax*? Maybe someone came to Nora's room after you left and mixed the vodka and *Xanax* into Nora's coffee when she wasn't paying attention."

That gave Iris an idea. She went over to her minibar and opened it. She saw four bottles of vodka inside. This made her wonder if all the fridges held the same contents, as she said, "I think I might have figured out how to prove your theory. Thanks for the help, son. I have to go now."

"All right. Please be careful."

"I will, dear," replied Iris before hanging up.

Afterward, she called the captain and said, "Sorry for bothering you again, captain. But I needed to ask you if all the mini fridges in the cabins contain the same contents."

"Yes, they do in fact. Why do you need to know?"

Iris spoke quickly, saying, "Thanks for the information. It's important regarding Nora's death, but I need to talk to the Inspector now. Bye," before hanging up.

IRIS STOOD OUTSIDE NORA'S CABIN. AS SHE KNOCKED ON THE door, she hoped the Inspector was still in the room investigating. A few minutes later, Iris got her answer: The door opened, and she saw Inspector Arabz. His face showed intrigue as he said, "I'm surprised to see you again so soon. Is everything all right?"

"Everything is fine, but I think I left something inside earlier. May I please come inside and look for it?"

The Inspector raised an eyebrow, saying, "Sure, no problem," before letting Iris inside.

Once inside, Iris waited until the Inspector closed the door to say, "I left nothing behind, but I said that in case someone was eavesdropping. I have a theory to prove that Nora was murdered if you follow me."

"I knew you hadn't dropped anything, but I was curious

to see what you were doing. So, lead the way. I want to see what this so-called theory is."

"Follow me then. I want to check out the mini fridge to see if it has four bottles of vodka. If it does, that means the bottle on the counter came from someone else's room."

"What an interesting idea. I didn't think of that. Let's go see if you're right."

A few moments later, Iris opened the mini fridge on the bar and discovered that all four bottles of vodka were there. Iris muttered, "Just what I thought. This mini fridge has four vodka bottles. So, the bottle on the counter came from somewhere else."

"I think that makes sense. However, I think you just made my job harder since this means Nora/Stacy was most likely murdered. Which means I should check out the crime scene again. Care to join me?"

Iris replied, "Yes, please," before they went over to the crime scene.

Iris scanned the crime scene again, trying to pay close attention to all the details. She wanted to figure out what had previously felt off to her. After a moment, she figured it out as she snapped her fingers and said, "Eureka. Now it all makes sense."

The Inspector turned to Iris as he said, "What did you find?"

Iris spoke eagerly, saying, "I think I just solved the mystery."

"Well, out with it then. Who is the guilty party?"

"I think I know who it is, but I need to have one more thing checked out first before I can be sure. Tomorrow morning, I'll have everything I need to state my case. Then I can tell you my theory from start to finish."

The Inspector looked intrigued and said, "You need to tell me who you think it is so I can protect you."

"Alright, fine. Here is who I think it is…"

After Iris had finished, the Inspector said, "That's an interesting theory you have, but how do we prove it?"

"If you can get the things I mentioned to you, I think we should be able to prove it."

"Alright, I'll try to get those things in the morning. Then, we'll be able to wrap up this case. In the meantime, stay on your guard. I don't want to see you get hurt."

"Thanks, Inspector, I will. I'll see you in the morning," said Iris before returning to her room.

ONCE INSIDE, IRIS CALLED UP HER SON AGAIN AND SAID, "Sorry to bother you again, Sammy, but I have one last favor. If possible, could you look into the VINs of our four remaining suspects? I want you to check and see if you can find any car reports showing that any of our four remaining suspects' cars underwent maintenance shortly after Inga Lagman was killed. I need it to help prove who the killer is tomorrow morning."

"I'll see what I can do, but you didn't give me much notice, Mom."

"I know Sammy. I'm sorry, but I'll make it up to you after the cruise. I'll bake your favorite brownies as a reward."

"All right, Mom. I'll call you tomorrow morning with the information."

"Thanks, son, you're the best. Love you, goodnight."

Iris heard Samuel say, "Love you too, night," before hanging up the phone. Afterward, she relaxed before going to bed.

80

Present Day
Thursday, August 15, 2024, 7:00 a.m.

Iris tossed and turned in her bed in an unsuccessful attempt to sleep. After a while, she gave up and got out of bed. The clock read 7:00 a.m. It was still much too early to expect a call from her son yet. So, to kill time, Iris ordered breakfast before grabbing some clean clothes and heading to the shower.

As the water fell on Iris, she slowly reviewed the clues she had found over the week. Once finished, she was convinced she'd be able to prove her theory later that morning. But she worried that something might go wrong. As Iris turned off the water, she hoped the Inspector would put up those key pieces of evidence so the killer couldn't tamper with them.

After drying off, Iris went to the kitchen and started a pot of coffee. A few moments later, she heard a knock at her door. That must be Joanne with her breakfast, she thought. Iris answered the door, but shock covered her face when she saw the killer standing outside her door holding a steak knife.

"Sorry to bother you this morning, but I wish to discuss something with you. I suggest you let me enter your cabin."

Iris didn't know what to do. If she closed the door, Tyler might try to kill Joanne, who was coming to bring her food at any moment. But if she let him into her room, he could kill her. Ultimately, she decided not to endanger Joanne and said, "Of course," before letting him inside.

After Tyler entered the room, he held a knife against Iris's back, guided her to sit at the kitchen bar, and warned, "Take a seat on the bar stool and refrain from any funny business."

Iris complied. After sitting down, she asked, "Why are you doing this, Tyler?"

Tyler spoke in an ugly, cruel tone, saying, "I saw you going in and out of Nora's room last night talking to the Inspector. I figured you either had or were close to figuring out I was behind it, so I need to silence you. But first, I want to know how you knew it was me."

Trying to stall for time, Iris said, "Well, the first clue was when you tried to kill me in Barbados. You dropped Sandy's business card when you took off. That clue allowed me to deduce that whoever it was had some connection to Sandy. But I wasn't sure how until I found the contract in Sandy's cabin that had his and Charles Underwood's signature. But I later recognized that the signature on the contract was not from Charles. It matched your handwriting when you gave me your phone number to give to my son. I also saw that it matched the forged suicide note you placed next to Nora's body in her cabin."

"Very clever of you, but how did you figure out my motive for these crimes?"

"Well, back in the past, Georgia had been having an affair with Charles, and he had met her at the strip club where she had worked at *Long Legs*. But you also worked there as her makeup artist. He had gotten Georgia pregnant, but she lost the baby. I had thought maybe she had done it since you used her liquid *Xanax, Alprazolam,* to commit the murders in her room. But when I searched her room, I found one of your earrings on the floor. One must have fallen out when you were in her bathroom. Plus, shortly after Stacy disappeared, someone saw Charles outside *Long Legs*. Many people thought he was breaking off an affair with Georgia, but that could have also been with you since you worked there as well. I think you plotted revenge for him dumping you back then. Am I right?"

Tyler laughed maliciously as he said, "Yes, you're right. He had promised to leave his wife for me for months. And when Stacy disappeared, I thought he would finally fulfill his promise. But he didn't. I blamed him and Stacy for ruining my happiness. So, when I found out Stacy was alive, I plotted my revenge for the tenth anniversary of when he broke my heart. I bought tickets for everyone on this cruise so that there would be plenty of people connected to the past in case my plan failed and I needed someone else to frame for the murder. Then I used my advertising skills to create those fake contests, saying that they won a free trip on this cruise to lure them here to set my plan into action."

"That's very clever, Tyler. But there is one thing that I don't understand."

"What's that? Your time is almost up."

"Why did you kill Inga Lagman?"

Tyler appeared shocked as he said, "How did you figure that out?"

"Well, everyone assumed Charles had killed her but couldn't prove it. When I talked to Nora yesterday before you killed her, she told me that Charles might have been the one to plot the killing of Inga, but he probably had someone else do the deed. After figuring out that you two were involved, I guessed that he might have convinced you that Inga had to die so he wouldn't go to jail for embezzlement, and that way, you two could stay together."

"Right once again. He was such a manipulator. He even got me to kill his intern, Clara's parents, because he suspected she had heard about us plotting to murder Inga. But he got what he deserved in the end. But that's enough chatter. It's time to say goodnight, Iris."

But just then, there was a knock at the door. Tyler spoke in a quite malicious tone, "Who is that? It had better not be the Inspector."

Iris felt goosebumps as she slowly muttered, "It's room service. I ordered breakfast earlier."

"Tell them to leave it outside."

"I have to sign the receipt to pay for the food."

Tyler groaned with frustration as he said, "Fine. Get up, but no funny business."

So, Iris slowly got up as Tyler led her to the door with the steak knife pressed against her neck. After slowly opening it, Iris said, "Thanks, Joan. It smells delicious."

Joanne gave a curious look as she said, "Glad to hear it, Miss. Here is the receipt for you to sign."

Iris awkwardly grabbed it, signed her name, and left a generous tip, hoping to leave a clue, along with saying her name wrong before returning it to Joanne.

"That's awfully generous of you, Miss Iris. Here's your food."

Iris attempted to give Joanne a desperate look before saying, "No problem, Joanne," before grabbing the tray and closing the door.

Iris hoped Joanne picked up on the subtle hints as Tyler led her back to the bar. After sitting down, he said, "Times up; you're going to drink some alcohol and *Xanax* and go to sleep. If you attempt any funny business, I will stab you to death with this steak knife. It's up to you."

"I'll take the *Xanax*, but can I choose the type of alcohol?"

Tyler groaned as he said, "Fine. Got to wrap this up. Open the mini fridge and take out whatever you prefer."

Iris only had one chance of this working and hoped she could pull it off. As she opened the mini fridge, she withdrew the bottle of white wine that was still full. Then, as quickly as possible, she grabbed it by its neck, swung around, and hit Tyler's head with it. The bottle burst on impact. And Tyler fell to the ground. She heard him curse out as she ran to the bathroom and locked the door. Then she pulled her phone out of her pocket and called the captain. As the phone rang, she heard Tyler pounding on the bathroom door, screaming obscenities at her. A few moments later, she heard the captain answer and say, "Good morning, Iris. Is everything all right?"

Iris spoke in a panic, saying, "No, it's not. I'm locked in my bathroom, and Tyler is trying to kill me. Please send help ASAP!"

"I'll call the Inspector, and we'll help as soon as possible. You could try to find a weapon and hide in the shower until we arrive."

"Good idea," Iris replied before hanging up. A moment later, Iris began looking through the bathroom for something to use as a weapon, just in case. She settled on hair spray before entering the shower and shutting the glass door. She held her weapon tight as she kept hearing Tyler ram into the bathroom door.

Time slowed down for Iris. And she panicked when Tyler busted the door open and said, "It ends here, witch," as he lunged to open the shower.

Iris pressed the button on the hairspray. It went directly into Tyler's eyes. He screamed in pain as he dropped the knife.

In the confusion, Iris shoved past Tyler, ran out of the shower, and down the hall towards the front door. As she went to open it, the door handle opened, and she spotted Inspector Arabz. Tears began rolling down her face as he said, "Where is he?"

Iris muttered, "In the bathroom. I sprayed him with hairspray to blind him."

The Inspector gave Iris a sympathetic look as he said, "Good job. I will take it from here."

Iris looked relieved as she watched the Inspector take off towards her bathroom.

81

Present Day
Thursday, August 15, 2024, 8:15 a.m.

Iris sat on her couch, sipping coffee, when her phone rang. Withdrawing it, she saw it was Samuel. In the morning's chaos, she had forgotten that he was supposed to call her this morning. As she answered the phone, she heard him say, "Good morning, Mom. There's positive news that I want to share. I discovered that after Inga's death, one person had their car worked on, and it was Tyler Reed."

"I know, dear. Tyler came and confronted me this morning. But I handled it, and the inspector arrested him about ten minutes ago."

"That's horrible. Did he hurt you?"

"No, dear. Although he tried to, I outsmarted him by hitting him with a wine bottle and spraying hairspray into his eyes before calling for the Inspector to come save me."

"That's amazing, Mom. I can't believe you outsmarted the killer like that. I'm glad that you're okay and that vile man has been arrested. I can't believe you tried to set me up with him."

"I am, too, dear. And I'm sorry, I didn't realize he was a killer at the time. But everything turned out okay. On a different note, can you send me that VIN information you found so I can show it to the Inspector later?"

"Sure thing, Mom. I'll send it once I get to work."

"Sounds good, Sammy. But I need to get going. I have some loose ends I need to tie up."

"Okay, Mom. Please be careful, I love you."

"No worries. Tyler is locked up, and I am no longer in danger. I want to talk to Jordan, Selina, and Georgia and tell them what happened so they can all move forward. Also, the ship got turned around, so the pickup time has changed. I'll call you later with more details. I love you too, bye." Iris waited until she heard Samuel say goodbye before hanging up.

IRIS KNOCKED ON JORDAN AND SELINA'S CABIN DOOR. AFTER A few moments, the door opened, and the couple looked surprised to see her. Iris said, "Sorry to bother you guys, but I have some good news to tell you. I figured out who killed Inga and your parents, Jordan, and they are in custody now."

Selina's face welled with tears as she pleaded, "Please tell me who did it and how you discovered the truth."

Jordan looked shocked and angry as he said, "Yes, please tell us who did this to our parents."

After Iris told her tale, Selina came up and hugged Iris as she said, "Thank you for telling me. Now I finally have peace, knowing that my mom's killer, as well as Jordan's parents, is going to face the justice they deserve."

Jordan also jumped in, saying, "Thanks for avenging our parent's death. It means a lot to us. I had no idea Charles was connected to my parent's death. Or why he thought I knew what he had plotted with Tyler about Inga."

"I'm glad to be of service. I hope you two can move forward now without worrying about the weight of the past. I wish I could tell you why Charles thought you knew, but knowing why he thought you knew is impossible. Try not to let it upset you anymore, but I have got to get going now. I got more people to speak to about what has happened."

The couple smiled and said, "Goodbye," before Iris took off.

Iris knocked on Georgia's door. A few moments later, Georgia appeared and said, "Good morning, sugar. How are you doing?"

Iris felt bad when she said, "Georgia, I have some bad news to tell you. Can I please come inside?"

Georgia looked concerned and said, "No, please tell me what you want to tell me."

"Well, the short version is that Tyler killed Charles, Sandy, Nora, Inga Lagman, as well as Jordan Mateo's parents."

Georgia looked shocked and said, "What, that can't be true? Please tell me you are joking."

Iris felt pity for Georgia as she explained how she figured it out. By the end, Georgia cried as she said, "I can't believe my best friend for the past ten years is such an evil human being. How could I have not seen it?"

"Criminals are very good at hiding their true identities. If they weren't, then crimes wouldn't go unsolved. Fortunately, he's been caught and can't harm anyone else again."

"That's true, sugar. But I think it will take a while for me to move past this. I think I need some time alone."

"I understand, dear. Please take care."

Georgia said somberly, "Thank you," before closing the door.

EPILOGUE

Present Day
Friday, August 16, 2024, 8:30 a.m.

Iris woke to her alarm going off. After yawning, she stretched and turned it off before climbing out of bed. Then she grabbed a fresh set of clothes she had left out from the night before and headed to the shower.

After a quick shower, Iris went and started a pot of coffee. While waiting for it to brew, she called room service to order breakfast. While she waited for it to arrive, Iris went around her room to check and see if she had forgotten to pack any of her belongings.

After a quick scan, Iris felt confident she hadn't forgotten anything. So, she returned to check on her coffee. A smile came to her face when she saw it was done. So, Iris went to grab a cup from the cabinet and poured some. After finishing her task, she sat on the couch to enjoy her coffee and reflect on her trip.

Iris couldn't believe all that had happened over this past week. She had met some fascinating people, and, most importantly, she had solved the mystery that had haunted her husband for years. The truth was shocking, but it brought closure and justice. She had almost gotten killed in the process, a risk she had been willing to take to uncover the truth. Henry wouldn't believe all of this if he were still alive. Then again, if he were still alive, he probably would have been the one investigating it instead. But after a moment, Iris laughed, realizing that wouldn't have changed anything except him worrying over her as they both tried to solve the case. She hoped she made Henry proud of being able to solve his cold case and this present one.

A few moments later, she heard a knock on her door and thought that was enough self-reflection as she went to answer the door. Joanne greeted her, saying, "Good morning, Iris. I brought your breakfast. I hope you enjoy yourself before you return home today. I apologize for not picking up on your hints yesterday about needing help. Please forgive me."

Iris gave Joanne a gentle smile as she said, "No problem, dear. Don't feel bad. It all worked out in the end, so no worries. It was nice getting to know you, Joanne. I hope you take care of yourself."

Joanne smiled and said, "I appreciate that a lot, Iris. Please sign this receipt so I can leave you to your breakfast."

Iris complied, and Joanne handed Iris the silver platter before taking off.

After breakfast, Iris placed the tray and her empty coffee cup in the sink. Then she checked the time on her phone. It read 9:40 a.m. It was time to leave. So, Iris grabbed her things before heading to the bridge.

On the bridge, Iris spotted all her new friends hanging out with their luggage. Georgia stood silently in the corner while Selina and Jordan stood beside each other, chatting. Iris went over and saw everyone one last time.

After chatting with everyone, Iris exchanged numbers and said they would try to stay in touch. Iris hoped maybe they could have more adventures in the future, minus a crazy killer involved. Jordan and Selina had mentioned getting married soon and offered to invite Iris to the wedding. But that

PERISH IN PARADISE

thought got interrupted as the ship landed at the Orlando pier. Iris followed her new friends off the ship, down the gangplank, and back to her hometown.

In the distance, she saw her children standing with a sign and a handsome-looking guy standing next to Samuel. Iris guessed that it was Ryan. She hoped he would treat her son well, but only time would tell. But for now, she was excited to tell all of them about her new friends now that the mystery was over. So, Iris headed over to greet them and do just that. She thought things weren't too bad as she let the SS Paradise fade into the background. She went to embrace her children and her son's new boyfriend with newfound hope in her heart.

(The End)

ACKNOWLEDGMENTS

My heartfelt thanks go out to my friends and family who stood by me as I poured my heart and soul into this book, rewriting it countless times and always believing in its potential to become a reality.

I want to thank my amazing cover artist, Courtny Bradley, for making both my eBook and physical book covers. She is also a debut cozy mystery writer with her book Death on Deck, which will be released on September 30, 2024.

I want to thank my editor, Dawn Baca, for her wonderful edit suggestions for my book. She is also an indie writer whose first book is Her Guarded Heart, part of the Letting Love In series, which is part of women's romance fiction.

I would like to thank my beta readers, Caitlyn L., Des M., Allison C., and Seth M., for their countless hours of reading my book and providing helpful feedback and edit suggestions that helped make it what it is today.

ABOUT THE AUTHOR

Christian is from the Midwest, and when he is not writing his latest mystery, he enjoys playing video games, binge-watching the newest crime show, or spending time with his family.

Milton Keynes UK
Ingram Content Group UK Ltd.
UKHW020754051024
449151UK00012B/574